# The Tangled Tower

## Reversed Retellings

## Book Two

by Tenille Berezay

The Tangled Tower



ISBN 9798994566732

Line by Line Publishing

Nevada, USA

First Edition

For the pleasers,

May you find direction through divine guidance,

the strength to say no when necessary,

and joy in saying yes.

# The World of Reversed Retellings

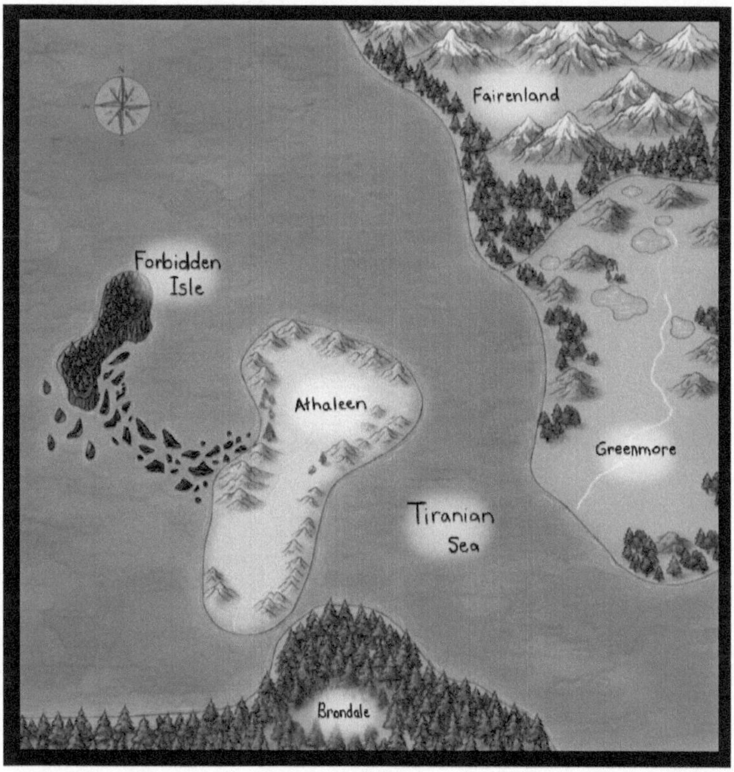

Fairenland
Forbidden Isle
Athaleen
Greenmore
Tiranian Sea
Brondale

# Chapter One

RANZEL NULLA hated his hands. In all honesty, they were rather filthy, bony, and battered. But that wasn't why the young child hated his hands.

He hated what they could do.

In a kingdom where magic was feared, Ranzel was magical. Not only was he a magic-bearer, but he also bore the weight of a very powerful, incredibly unique type of magic. It was a heavy load for a child still in his ninth year. To Ranzel, it seemed the weight grew as he did, a burden he could never set aside or share with another.

Ranzel's family had abandoned him several years past. The young boy had a few memories of a

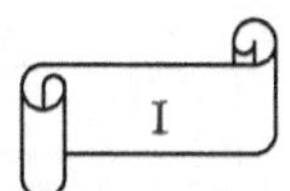

younger brother and a quiet mother, but as time moved him farther and farther away from his life *before* magic, the memories grew dimmer and dimmer. He lived in the *after* now—the aftermath of discovering his power while playing in a sparse yard with his toddler brother. The after that began with his mother's heartbroken expression as his ability was manifested. The distraught expression on her face—so different from her typical loving smiles—would live with Ranzel eternally. But smiles were for before, and Ranzel didn't cling to memories because he was too busy clinging to survival. In the before, he had had a home, love. In the after, he was an urchin, starving and despised.

After years on the street, he'd learned to be cautious and trust no one. He'd also found value in his magic, though he still hated it. Hated what it had lost him and what little it gave him in return.

Ranzel turned his focus from his offending hands and back to the market. Like any good thief, he was looking for a mark. Unlike a regular thief, he wasn't searching for a wealthy, distracted shopper but a nondescript younger citizen—someone with a

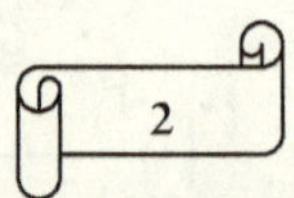

maneuverable build, forgettable features, and clothing that spoke of middle-class employment.

Finally, Ranzel found the perfect scapegoat. He watched the young man dart through the market, hurriedly buying a basketful of ingredients, and head back the way he had come. Judging by his uniform, he was a servant, a runner for a visiting lord. The perfect unremarkable mark.

Ranzel stared at the man's retreating form, memorizing his features before stepping into the alley. His skin tingled as power moved through him like an internal breeze. The shifting magic was practically instantaneous. Between one heartbeat and the next, Ranzel became taller, older, and a perfect replica of the young man.

Perfectly disguised, Ranzel stepped from the alley and searched out a new target, this time a more traditional one.

The thievery went off without a hitch. Ranzel brushed up against the wealthy man and, with a flick of his wrist, stole one of the money bags at his waist. Ranzel had learned not to be too greedy because greed only brought attention from the victims *and*

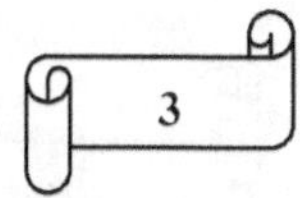

from the other street urchins. Of course, the victims took exception to someone stealing their possessions and became angry in a loud way that alerted the guards and threatened imprisonment. The street urchins took exception to someone thieving in their territory and became angry in a quiet way that alerted no one but promised painful retribution. Because of this, Ranzel avoided any and all attention.

Yes, in Ranzel's world, you didn't want to be noticed. Ranzel's short lifetime had taught him that *all* attention was negative. He never again wanted to be *seen*. It had only ever brought him trouble. Ranzel's goal was to remain in the background, stay as invisible as possible, steal only to survive, and slip away before anyone could question the means of his easy success.

Working toward his ultimate goal of absolute obscurity, Ranzel ducked back into the alley and turned back into himself—a seemingly ordinary, starving orphan.

But he wasn't going to starve this night.

Turning to the market, warm meat pies on his mind, Ranzel practically ran into a cloaked figure.

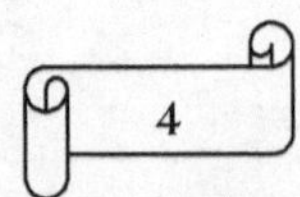

The figure calmly lifted the hood of his cloak back, revealing long flowing hair, small protruding eyes, and smooth yellow skin. His physical attributes clashed, not seeming to fit quite right on his face. They were all mismatched and wrong. Old and young. Harsh and kind. Attractive and hideous. The disjointed features reminded Ranzel of the loving, yet horrified look he'd last seen on his mother's face as she abandoned him. It was unnatural.

But the unnatural didn't scare Ranzel. His life was full of the unnatural.

However, the man's words terrified Ranzel, as—in a surprisingly clear voice—he said, "I saw your magic, young one."

Ranzel's mind quickly began calculating possible escape routes. He made a move to dart forward between the man and the stone wall. The man simply stepped aside to let him pass.

The cloaked man's action caused Ranzel to hesitate, and he looked at the man again. If the man wasn't going to capture him in anger, then surely he was disgusted or terrified of Ranzel's magic. The young boy studied the inexplicable face, expecting

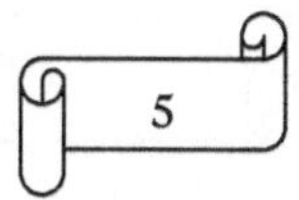

him to turn away. To abandon or abuse him. But, instead, the man spoke. His words charted an entirely new course for Ranzel's life.

"I'm Mage Zelroth," he said. "Unlike so many others, I appreciate your talent. Your magic. An ability such as yours should be developed. Come with me, and I will help you."

In disbelief, Ranzel listened to the mage's words. For the first time in years, he considered a future beyond his next meal. The mage continued, "I can make you into a powerful man. Together, we can create a world where your magic isn't feared, but celebrated. You never need steal again, never need be hungry. Come with me. I vow to protect you."

The mage held out a strong, pale hand. The boy studied the outstretched palm, inched slowly forward, and tentatively slid his hated hand into the mage's promising one.

TEN YEARS LATER…

The night began like any other. Mage Zelroth secured his workspace and sought out Ranzel in the

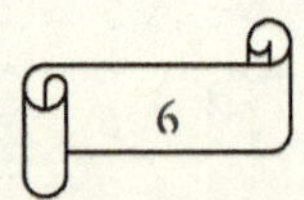

uppermost level of the tower. There, he ensured Ranzel and, more importantly, Ranzel's magic were prepared for their nightly task.

Ranzel quickly assured the mage he had rested and felt stronger than ever. Pleased, Zelroth placed a hand on Ranzel's shoulder. It was a noteworthy attempt at a connection. The mage rarely touched Ranzel, claiming Ranzel's physical magic was diminished by contact.

"Always remember to keep up your strength, apprentice,"Zelroth said, releasing Ranzel's shoulder after offering a too-tight squeeze. Ranzel fought the urge to rub his shoulder, unwilling to offend his master. Heedless of Ranzel's discomfort, Zelroth looked out over the moonlit isle and continued, "Soon we will have gained enough influence." His long fingers curled around a pendant-like bottle attached to a tether hanging from his neck. He clasped it tightly, his hold jangling the other eleven. "Soon we will be able to continue in our plan to bring the respect for, and power of, magic to every kingdom." The mage dropped the tether and tucked all eleven under his robe.

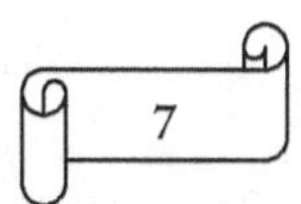

Turning, he examined Ranzel as he made his final declaration. "Soon you will be able to leave this tower."

Ranzel, always quiet, only nodded in agreement. The mage watched him with small, dark eyes.

Truthfully, Ranzel didn't mind the physical toll his magic took every night. He didn't mind the essence of himself he had given to his master to create the twelve tethering potions the mage wore like a talisman around his neck. He didn't mind using his magic to transport the royalty here. He didn't mind living stuck in the tower. He didn't mind because all of these things would give him what he really wanted. Or at least what Zelroth *told* him he wanted—a chance to fulfill his magical duty.

"I must see to my duty," Mage Zelroth finally said, still watching Ranzel.

"To you, my magic is freely given," Ranzel replied.

It was an oath he often repeated, a pledge Mage Zelroth had earned by freeing him from a life of fear, offering him a future, and bringing him to this tower. To this isle of protection.

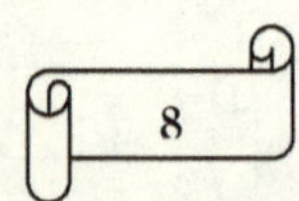

Satisfied by Ranzel's words of devotion, Zelroth checked the twelve pendants and disappeared to his nightly negotiations. Ranzel watched from the tower's highest parapet. From there, he could see Zelroth glide through the woods to a stone structure in the distance. Ranzel had never been to the structure, staying safe in the tower, but the mage assured him it was a place of gathering, proving, and compromise.

As the clock grew closer to midnight, Ranzel descended the stairs to his living area. This level of the tower was Ranzel's favorite place because it had no interior walls, just a large, circular, open space filled with all of the comforts of life: inviting seating, a warming fire, well-used books, a partial dirt floor, greenery flourishing, a trickling stream of water, and a large stone-arched window with an amazing view.

There, he pulled his favorite wooden chair to the stone ledge, leaned against the cold rock, and waited.

The midnight hour came. Ranzel felt the now familiar pull on his magic, and twelve princes appeared. Ranzel could just see them through the foliage of the trees.

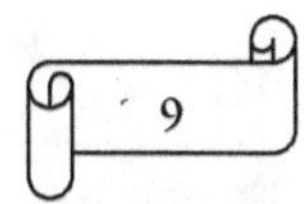

Zelroth assured him the tower was far enough away to keep him safe, but close enough for the reach of his magic. Transporting the princes took a great toll, and Ranzel lay on the cold stone as his magical strength was sapped from him. The princes moved into boats and drifted out of sight, followed by an unseen current of power.

Ranzel's power and the princes were mixed in the mage's tethers. As Zelroth explained, Ranzel supplied the power and physical connection, but his master controlled it with the pendants. The magic was contained in the tethers like a spell locked in an artifact, but—unlike an artifact—when the power was accessed, it affected the originator of the power.

Usually, Ranzel fell asleep at the window, but on this night, things went very differently.

After only a short time at the window, Ranzel felt a snap of power, a lessening of the current traveling to the isle below. Then there was another snap and another. With each break, Ranzel felt a rush of energy…and a rush of dread. When the last connection broke, Ranzel stood staring through the trees, seeing little and understanding even less.

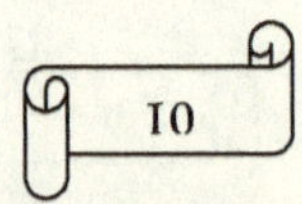

Suddenly, Zelroth appeared, dripping wet and clutching an empty potion vial in his right hand. A relocation potion. A potion he only ever used in emergency situations.

"What has happened?" Ranzel said, his voice pitched high with anxiety.

"I must go warn the other mages," Zelroth said, gathering items into a bag. He was flushed, and his protruding eyes darted around, looking wild and trapped. He threw his empty vial aside, murmuring what seemed to be a list to himself. "Larger transportation potion, meet with the others, Captain of Athaleen, secure potions." With one last look around the tower, the mage turned to Ranzel, his dark eyes piercing.

"You will remain here until I return. Yes?"

Ranzel nodded, but this wasn't enough for the mage, who lunged forward and grabbed him by the collar. "Look at me, apprentice. You will stay here—in the tower—no matter how long my absence."

"Yes," Ranzel agreed. "I vow it."

But the mage didn't loosen his hold. He only pulled Ranzel closer, his fingers claw-like in their

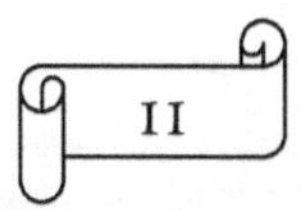

desperate grip. "And you will not enter my workspace. Ever. No matter the reason."

Ranzel studied his master, the master who had saved him, taught him, and prepared him for more. Then he promised:

"To you, my magic, and my word, is freely given."

# Chapter Two

PRINCESS FLYNN of Athaleen watched the sails of the ship disappear into the horizon. As they faded from view, the healing root she had so desperately searched for dropped from her hand to roll across the newly-built planks of the dock.

They had left her.

A stiff wind pushed at her back, practically propelling her from the dock toward the choppy sea. The trade winds had arrived. Which meant, even when they realized she was missing, they couldn't return. Not for some time.

A normal princess might have succumbed to a fit of tears. Or curled up in despair.

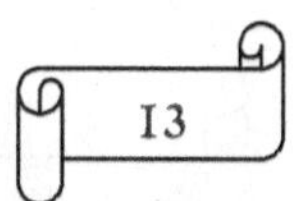

Flynn was not normal.

The first thing she felt was concern. Lady Smythe was going to go crazy with worry. And guilt. It was for the lady and her weak stomach that Flynn had left the ship amid all the crazy bustle of departure to find the healing herb. On their voyage over, Lady Smythe—the captain's young wife—had spent most of the time sick in her chambers. Due to her being the only other woman on their excursion, she and Flynn had become fast friends. Once Flynn recalled the healing herb her sister Flora had once told her about, she'd rushed to procure some before their departure.

On reflection, Flynn should have informed someone other than her friend of her mission. Especially as Lady Smythe's color had already been fading and she'd been determined to rest before the winds and the open ocean besieged her once again. Flynn should have told one of her fellow soldiers, if not the captain.

Flynn's second thought was for those soldiers and the captain. Would they be angry? Or would they be afraid of the king's wrath? Would they try to return? As the wind gusted around her feet, she prayed they wouldn't. It was too dangerous. And she was safe. Right?

The time Flynn and the king's entourage had spent on The Forbidden Isle had made her quite familiar with its resources…and its dangers. Flynn reached for the bow at her back, finding comfort in holding the weapon in her hands. She also had a water skin and a small supply of rations.

Flynn assessed her options. She could go back to the stone arena. It had shelter and a few rusty, questionable weapons left behind after their purging. But it was also a hotbed for wild creatures. Probably not the best place to set up camp. Besides, it was near the opposite side of the isle, a distance that she could easily cover in a day.

Flynn didn't have a whole day. She glanced at the purpling sky. She had an hour.

Turning her attention to the shore, she scanned the water's edge. The boat had been docked here for over a month as the entourage explored the isle. Surely, resources were left behind. But her exploration of the shore brought her little: a small hatchet, an empty barrel, a brightly colored shell.

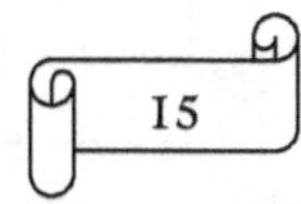

Her brother, Humphrey, and Tesha would be proud to know that their men had so thoroughly cleared the area. Before Tesha had become a royal advisor, she'd been captain of the guard and trained these men. Now, Prince Humphrey was captain and every bit as strict as his predecessor.

Unless Tesha was involved. Then he was indulgent. So indulgent.

It was rather entertaining watching the two most intense soldiers in the king's army go soft around each other. Flynn had always looked up to her brother, following his footsteps into the army and training with the same legendary zeal. Now, she found she admired him even more as he coddled his wife. Tesha was the most complete person Flynn had ever met. But now, seeing her in love, Flynn realized that love made a complete person even more whole. More fulfilled.

Maybe someday, Flynn would search for that fulfillment, but not today. Today, she was stranded.

As she took up the hatchet and began building herself a shelter for the night, she realized she wasn't at all upset. She was…excited. Another adventure.

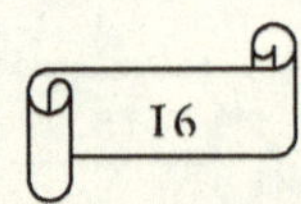

Flynn hadn't known she loved adventure until she went on one with Tesha. Sure, she'd gone on small adventures before with the army, even smaller ones with her siblings. Those felt different because she was following, appeasing the commands of her leaders or the whims of her sisters. The first adventure to the isle with Tesha had felt more like a partnership. Tesha asked her opinion, sought her guidance, listened to her ideas. Tesha never wanted to be pleased or appeased. She wanted truth. And Flynn found she loved that freedom. And the excitement.

Adventure suited the princess, felt less demanding than everything else in her life.

How grateful she was, she hadn't backed out on her commitment to join Tesha and strive to free her brothers from a horrible curse. She'd joined on an impulse, to please the captain. At her father's dismay and Humphrey's pleading, she'd almost rescinded her vow. It was her mother, Queen Abriana's, quiet suggestion to seek the Maker's guidance and choose accordingly that had convinced Tesha to follow her heart.

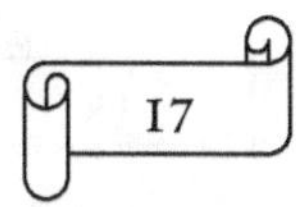

And the Maker seemed to lead her from adventure to adventure. First, helping break a curse. Next, joining the entourage on their exploration. And now, surviving an abandoned isle.

PRINCESS FLYNN OF ATHALEEN skipped into the meadow. She'd been alone on the isle for almost three weeks. She'd experienced the highs and lows of isolation.

High—no one to please. Her choices were her own. Low—no one to please. No one to serve. No one to receive praise and validation and love from.

High—danger around every corner. Flynn was becoming a very seasoned warrior. Low—difficulty sleeping with lurking dangers.

High—time to reflect on who she was and what she wanted. Low—time to reflect on what she didn't like about herself.

Last night had been a low. Crying silent tears by the fire outside of a mostly secure shelter, she had allowed herself to feel the lowest of the low. But not today.

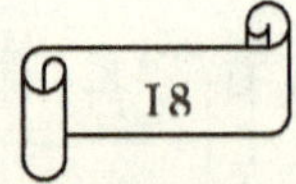

Today, she was happy about her situation.

Not many princesses would have been happy about Flynn's reality. Stuck on an isle, coping with a scarcity of food, sleeping in a make-shift shelter, being alone, and...

...being stalked by an animal.

Flynn was overjoyed.

Keeping the jovial bounce in her step, she casually pulled her bow free and notched an arrow. Not missing or skipping a beat, she spun as the creature charged. Flynn fired, hitting the large lizard-like animal between the eyes.

It dropped with a definitive thump.

Flynn trotted over to the animal and propped a leg on its carcass, victorious. "Looks like you're dinner, my overlarge friend," she said with a smirk.

She was so busy rejoicing over her kill that she didn't notice the creature's friend slinking up behind her until it was almost too late.

The second lizard's tail knocked her from the carcass and flat onto her back. In that moment, Flynn considered that this was probably her lowest low. If she didn't get eaten.

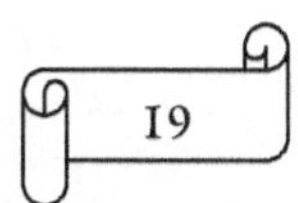

She expertly rolled away, narrowly avoiding the animal's razor-sharp claws as it pounced. Pulling an old, repaired dagger from her belt, she turned to face the angry creature.

As it charged her, she offered a quick prayer that the dagger would prove effective, slid under the animal's snapping jaw, and struck upward in a vicious attack to the beast's throat. This lizard died just as quickly and dramatically as the first, but perished pinning the princess to the ground.

With a few creative oaths and angry kicks, Flynn was free.

She stayed sprawled on the ground, catching her breath. She was lucky. She was alive. She was invincible! She pumped a victorious fist in the air, then dropped it onto the blood-soaked grass beside her, exhausted.

The princess stayed flat on her back. As her heart rate slowed, she surveyed the sky and surrounding forest. That's when she saw it, the corner of a tower. It shimmered in the light, fading in and out of view. But it was there, hidden, but there.

The tower was real.

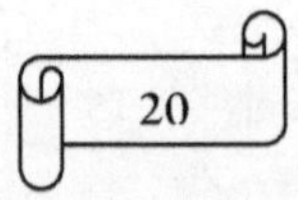

The king's entourage had spent much of the first two weeks on the isle searching for this mysterious tower. Both Tesha and Flynn had spotted it on their original adventure. However, their searching had proven futile. Flynn had pushed the expedition leader to keep searching, but he had finally convinced her to focus her efforts on building the dock and exploring the tangible.

But now, she'd found the very real, very *tangible* tower.

The tower was magically made. Flynn knew this not because the structure was anything fancy or special, but because it was so well hidden in the forest, the stone practically blending into the trees. Stone shouldn't blend into trees, or sky, or anything and everything around it. It was purposefully elusive. Yet, somehow, she had found it.

She approached the structure carefully, studying it with enthusiastic interest. The tower was taller than any building she had ever seen. As she circled it, she judged its size to be about twenty paces across and six stories high. There wasn't a door or any point of entry on the bottom that she could find. Far out of

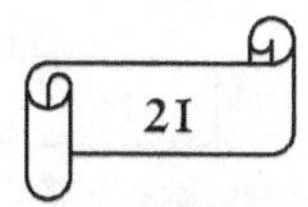

reach—about midway up the tower—was a tiny window. Near the top of the tower, there were larger arched windows, and at the very top, castle-like battlements.

As Flynn squinted at the tower, she saw movement through a window. There, but gone in a second. Humming to herself, she placed one hand on the tower as if to reassure herself it was real. The state of her hand shocked her a bit, covered in cracking dried blood. After her battle she was a mess, but she didn't want to risk losing sight of the tower again.

Settling on a plan, she removed her shoes and stowed them in her quiver, wedging them between the arrows.

It took her a few tries, but Flynn finally managed to figure out how to hook her feet in the grooves between the rock.

She quickly scaled the outer wall, tapping into tree-climbing skills left over from her youth. The thrill of discovery pushed her tired limbs up. Higher and higher. She finally reached the small window and pulled herself to a crouch on the small ledge.

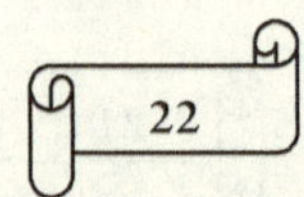

Inside the tower was a large open space filled with barrels and crates. A storage area. On the far wall, a winding stair was built into the wall. It spiraled up to the windowed area and down to the lower levels.

Flynn chose up, creeping to the narrow stairs on agile, dancing feet. The adventure of it all made calming her racing heart and twitching feet difficult. Upon reaching a hatch, she paused to steady her breathing and sharpen her awareness. With a steady hand, she cracked open the door.

An unexpected sight met her eyes.

It was a living space. A magical, perfect living space. It was like the most beautiful natural setting and the most exquisitely fashionable suite had been blended tastefully together. There were plants everywhere, large flowering trees and bushes spaced along the way with vines trailing around the room. The sound of running water was coming from somewhere. Near the center of the room was a roaring fire casting light over plush furnishings. An overlarge rug covered much of the stone floor, books were scattered here and there, and signs of life were nowhere.

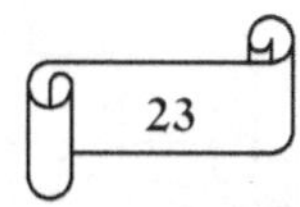

Flynn eased through the opening. With a slack jaw and wide eyes, she scanned the space. The source of the water became apparent as she looked behind her to discover almost half the room looked like an idyllic meadow. Grass on the floor, a gurgling stream, and delightful ground cover.

The princess lowered her hand to touch the tiny, soft flowers. She was enchanted.

A sound came from up above, bringing Flynn back to reality. She readied her bow, aiming it toward another rising staircase. A foot appeared on the stairs, then another, until an entire person came into view. An entire man. A man who was lean and attractive with light blonde hair and soft brown eyes.

At his full appearance, Flynn froze. Perhaps because the Maker stayed her hand, sparing his life. Perhaps because she was starving for human interaction. Perhaps because she found him immediately fascinating and attractive.

At least he was, until he saw Flynn, jumped, and with a yelp, changed into the last person the princess expected.

# Chapter Three

TO SAY THAT RANZEL was surprised to find another person in his tower would be an understatement. A person in his personal space was startling enough. But this person?

This person would be an unexpected find in a bustling city center, a blood-soaked battlefield, or even a manicured garden. Yet, somehow, she looked as if she partially belonged in all three.

She was slight. Her feet were bare and small and her hands were narrow and delicate. Full, dark hair was contained by an interlocking network of braids, and hypnotic hazel eyes stared at him with open interest. She had a brown cloak tossed over one

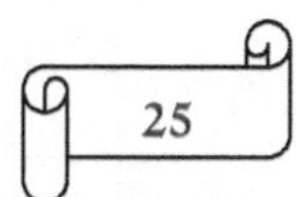

shoulder, a stained dagger secured in a belt at her trim waist, and a bow accompanied by a quiver of arrows slung across her back.

All of these details were interesting, possibly even noteworthy, but the smattering of blood across her face and trailing over her hands claimed Ranzel's attention—that and the arrow pointing in his direction.

He should have run. Darted right back up the stairs, found an emergency potion, and disappeared. That's probably what Zelroth would have wanted him to do. Probably. But despite all of Zelroth's instruction on how to keep people from discovering and accessing the tower, Ranzel's master had never instructed him on what to do if you found an intriguing girl *in* the tower.

As the seconds ticked by, Ranzel found himself inching down the remaining stairs, arrested by the gore marking her body and her consuming stillness. She was odd. She was beautiful. She was captivating. She was a mess.

"Are you injured?" he couldn't help but ask.

"Am I..." the girl spluttered. "You are...I am."

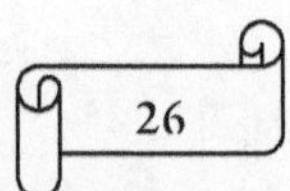

He waited, raising one brow. It wasn't until the movement felt unnatural that he remembered he had taken on her appearance. This was a common reaction when he was startled, but surely as disconcerting to her as the blood was to him.

He looked down at his hands seeing her hands, even the blood upon them. He was really quite talented in his illusions. Now, Ranzel could have changed back to himself, but Zelroth's warnings sounded in his head.

What if this girl were searching for him? Though no one knew what he looked like. He'd been in the tower for years. What if he dropped his illusion, she saw what he looked like, and she told someone? All anonymity gone. But who would she tell? And why? He'd done nothing wrong. Well, maybe creating the tethers and then forcing the princes into negotiations was wrong, but necessary.

Ranzel could always hide, changing into someone else.

After a flurry of mental deliberations, Ranzel made up his mind. He would stay. This was his tower, his home for years. She was the intruder, no

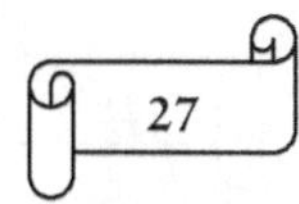

matter how unlikely or strangely attractive. But he wouldn't show his true self just yet. Some perverse need to know this stranger's reaction to the experience of seeing *him* as *her* held Ranzel back. He stopped at the base of the stairs, watching her gawk and stammer.

Finally, she gathered words together and exclaimed, "You're me!" Instead of sounding horrified, she sounded thrilled.

Now Ranzel was gaping, his replicated jaw dropping open. And it lowered even further, widening comically as Flynn threw her hesitation and weapon aside and rushed toward him.

Poking at his face and smoothing his/her hair, she exclaimed, "Wow, I really am something. What a battle-worn disaster! But not bad, not too bad." She pulled on a braid, then grabbed Ranzel's wrist, twisting his arm this way and that, saying, "Considering all I've been through, I'm looking positively awesome!"

Without thought, Ranzel morphed back into himself. But the girl didn't retreat. Instead, she stretched his cheeks and twisted his hair.

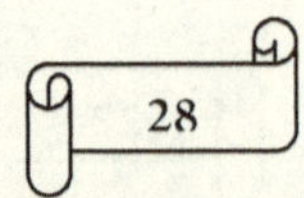

"This is amazing! Can you teach me how to do it!?"

Straightening his tunic, Ranzel tried to find some dignity and stepped away from her, knocking his foot into the stairs and almost falling backward.

With a sharp, casual movement, Flynn caught him, pulled him upright, and said, "Well, can you?"

Determined to stop the unraveling of a situation spinning wildly out of control, Ranzel said, "I am a mage." He pointed at himself. "I'm not manipulating power around me. I was born with it *inside* me." At best, he hoped his words would scare Flynn so much she'd flee. At worst, he expected them to create that familiar, horrified hatred in her eyes.

Instead, she made herself at home. Casually gathering her discarded bow and arrow, she unnotched the arrow and returned it to her quiver. From the quiver, she pulled out…shoes? "I'm disappointed, mage. I would love to be able to do what you can do." But she didn't sound disappointed, and she didn't act intimidated. Pulling a chair from the table, she sat and began putting them on.

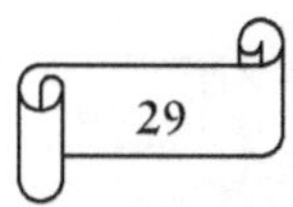

"What are you doing, girl?" he demanded. At least he tried to sound demanding, but shock and misuse made his voice weak.

"Girl!?" Flynn snapped upright. "I'm not a girl, I'm a—"

Flynn stopped herself from admitting she was a princess. Of course, she couldn't tell him that. This seemingly unthreatening mage was likely involved in her brother's curse. How involved, she'd love to find out, but she needed to be strategic. Her brother, Humphrey, said she was too bold, too brave. So he'd taught her how to fight, how to get her opponent off guard. How to attack when the time was right. How to be patient and wait for the right opportunity.

Flynn needed to be careful, but she also hated lying. In her opinion, lies wasted time. If people were honest, problems could be faced and solved a lot more efficiently.

So, she told a partial truth. "I'm a woman. A soldier of Athaleen."

Ranzel darted to the window, looking around as if he expected to see an entire army below. "Where are the rest?"

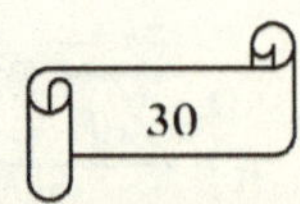

"It's just me," Flynn said, then mumbled a curse under her breath—so much for being careful. Dang her impetuous nature. "Are you alone?" she demanded.

"Of course. Always," the mage said, still staring down at the meadow below the tower.

Flynn sensed honesty in his quick, dismissive answer and sighed in relief. Thankfully, he was alone, too. She should have never admitted she was alone.

Tesha always said you should have backup, and if you don't, you should *pretend* to. Which was like lying, so maybe…

Flynn shook her head. This was why she didn't like politics. She'd leave those to her sister Ericka, who seemed to love them. Strange princess.

"What are *you* doing here?" Ranzel demanded, and this time his voice was strong, sharpened by stress.

Here, Flynn told the complete truth, hoping she could build a rapport. "I was left by accident, but now my people can't return because of the trade winds."

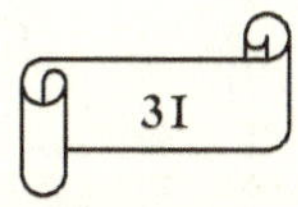

"How did you find the tower?" Ranzel asked, running his hands through his hair and looking very nervous and twitchy and young.

"Don't fret about your magic failing, my friend. I only saw it because I was at an odd angle. You see, there was this lizard..."

Flynn proceeded to tell the story of the lizards attacking. Casually sharing a tale of near-death wasn't new to Flynn, and she did love a good story. She was good at telling one, too.

When Ranzel began to show interest, she kept going. Telling of all the thrilling battles, nerve-wracking attacks, and fights for survival that had occurred since her abandonment.

Eventually, even the princess lost herself in the excitement of the story, sitting comfortably at the table as she swung her arms in exaggerated movements. Apparently, Ranzel relaxed too because by the end of the tellings, they were both completely engaged, sitting at the table, leaning toward one another.

It was the start of what Flynn hoped would be the discovery and the adventure of a lifetime.

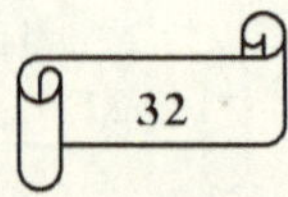

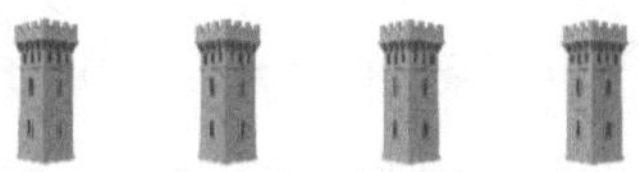

THE NEXT MORNING, Flynn sprang from her bed, excited for the day. Today, she would get more information from the mage. Perhaps his name.

Last night, after she had told the stories of her days alone on the isle, described the many creatures she had found, and detailed the many creative ways she had dispatched those monsters, she had been overcome with exhaustion.

Still completely off guard and too overwhelmed by the woman, Ranzel had silently watched her snatch a pillow from a plush chair, tuck herself in next to the fire, and sleep.

Then, Ranzel had sat across the room, trying to wrap his head around what had happened. And *how* it had happened. And *why* he had allowed it to happen. After staring into the flames for a long while, Ranzel watched the soldier sleep—her face vibrant even in repose. Then he had quietly made his way upstairs where he slept little, but thought a lot.

Flynn wasn't a fool. She slept with her stained dagger at the ready. She had feigned sleep for a time

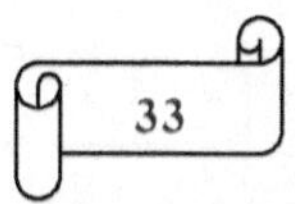

to see what the mage would do. If he attacked or attempted to throw her from the tower, she would learn much about him. But he didn't throw her out or attack. Or anything. He left her alone.

Which is just what Flynn expected. If she acted like she belonged in his world and was comfortable there, he'd let her stay. And she'd get her answers. Her plan was working perfectly.

The princess scrubbed herself clean at the gently flowing creek. She sat for a time in prayerful contemplation, enjoying the peaceful space. For whatever reason, after weeks of living on edge, Flynn felt safe. She suspected she shouldn't, but she did seem to be *safer.*

Prepared for a day of adventure, Flynn regained her feet and noticed a pleasant smell coming from a lower level.

Following the smell, she found herself on the same level as the tiny window she'd accessed to get into the tower. She tracked the powerful scent around the storage barrels and stacks of crates to find Ranzel in a somewhat hidden area. It was actually rather spacious and had all the necessities of a kitchen.

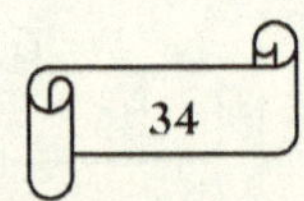

There, Ranzel was cooking something over a fire. It smelled amazing, so she inched closer to get a peek. He didn't move away, but his body stiffened. Flynn ignored his unease. "Are you cooking?" she asked.

He looked at her incredulously. Ranzel wasn't used to small talk. He wasn't used to talk at all, and Flynn questioning the obvious made him very concerned for the soldier's mental health.

"Who else would cook?" he said, giving her a sideways glance.

Unknowingly, he had answered Flynn's real question, which was: were they truly alone. She felt she needed to verify one more time before she dropped her guard.

In fact, they *were* very much alone in the tower. Ranzel had lived most of his life alone. He was so used to being alone, he didn't know there was a word to describe the aching hole in his chest when he thought of other people. He just thought it was a state of being.

With Flynn's overbearing, chatty personality, Ranzel was *less* alone than he had ever been, while

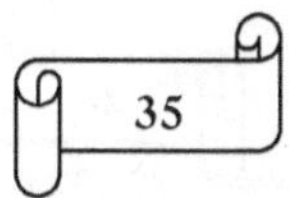

Flynn was *more* alone than she'd ever been. Having been raised with nine siblings and being part of an army, the princess was accustomed to being surrounded. Having been raised with a master who only talked to teach, the mage was accustomed to being left alone. Being in a tower with one other person was an adjustment for both.

"What is your name, mage?" Flynn asked as she searched the nearby shelves for plates.

Ranzel skimmed around her, grabbing a bowl and a plate from a higher shelf. "Ranzel," he muttered under his breath.

"Ranzel," she mused. "Ranzel. Interesting. I like it. Mine is Flynn." With introductions done, she took the bowl from the table, filled it with the delicious smelling food, said grace, and dug in with gusto.

Ranzel joined her at the table, considering.

Considering throwing her out. Considering escaping to his chamber and locking the door. Considering her unorthodox view of life. Considering the chaos she had brought to his orderly world and, mostly, considering why he liked it.

# Chapter Four

ONCE FLYNN'S STOMACH was full, she pushed the bowl away and began unpinning and unbraiding her hair.

Oblivious to Ranzel gawking at her, she said, "Tell me about yourself, Ranzel. Have you always lived in this tower in the middle of an isle that is literally forbidden?"

"Yes," Ranzel said, disarmed by the sight of her so casually unbraiding and rebraiding her hair at his table.

Flynn didn't consider it strange. She may have been a princess, but she trained as a soldier. Captain Tesha hadn't allowed special treatment, so when

Flynn traveled with the army, she did much of her personal care in front of others.

Ranzel was *not* used to seeing another person going about their personal business. Especially a person with hair so beautiful, so shiny. All of a sudden, it was highly uncomfortable sharing his space with another human.

Especially one he didn't know what to do with.

He supposed she could stay with him until her ship returned. But what if his master returned before then? He recalled Zelroth muttering something about Athaleen that fateful night he'd disappeared. And Flynn was a soldier of Athaleen. Frowning, he ran a finger over a chip in the table. Ranzel was unpracticed in making decisions. Every choice he made for years had been guided by Zelroth, motivated by duty. Only now Zelroth wasn't here, and his sense of duty caused him to feel oddly protective of this Flynn woman.

Ranzel was so busy considering Flynn and the issues her presence brought that he didn't notice that she was gawking at him. And had been for some time.

"Ranzel, I was in jest," she finally sputtered. "But you are serious. You have *always* lived here in this tower? Alone?"

"Most of my life," Ranzel admitted. "When I was a boy, I lived in Fairenland."

"I would have chosen the tower as well," she said, working to keep the conversation going by keeping it light. But she noted he didn't mention anything about being alone. "That's a cold, miserable place."

"Cold in many ways," he mumbled, speaking of his homeland.

"How so?" she asked, keeping her gaze trained on her hair and her voice casual.

"What do you think of magic?" Ranzel asked.

His response surprised Flynn. He was actually pushing the conversation, even deepening it. She responded with open candor. "Very little. I used to think it was a myth. Or something that was lost to time. But yours isn't the first magic I have seen."

Flynn finger-combed another braid, thinking of her last trip to the isle. Remembering the mage who had trapped her brothers and other princes here and forced them to fight night after night. He had been

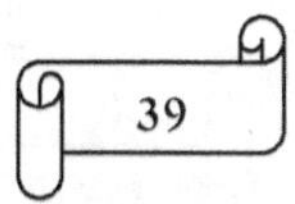

syphoning magic from them, a magic they hadn't even known they had. A magic that apparently *all* royals had.

So, Flynn was magic, too. With this sudden realization, she said, "I suppose magic, like people, can be good or bad. What do you think of magic?"

"That it is feared." Ranzel answered, his eyes on Flynn's fingers as she deftly tied off a long, twisted strand of hair.

"I suppose it is," she said dismissively. "Because people misuse it." Flynn paused, questioning how far to push this mage, who may or may not have been involved with her brothers' abuse. "Magic shouldn't be used to curse people, to force them into actions of any type, especially dangerous ones. It shouldn't be used to control people. Ever."

"So it should be outlawed?" Ranzel said, Flynn's words creating in him a volatile mix of anger and guilt.

"If used to control," Flynn said, keeping her voice calm and continuing to casually twist her hair.

The mage's temper flared. Teetering on the edge of control, Ranzel accused Flynn, saying, "You

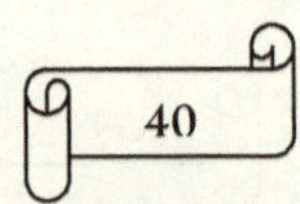

believe that because magic *can* be bad that magicians should be hunted and eradicated?"

"What! No!" Flynn exclaimed, dropping the braid she had almost finished fixing. "That would be horrible? Is that done in Fairenland?"

He stood, his chair screeching, and paced to the fire. Poking aggressively at the coals, he said, "Practically, magicians are despised. Looked down on. Thrown out."

"You were thrown out," she stated, trying to keep the pity from her voice.

"Yes."

"You were despised."

"Yes."

"You are a magician."

"Y—no."

"Ah-ha!" Flynn said, finishing her hair with a flourish. "Of course, you are. You turned into me. If that's not the best kind of magic, I don't know what is!"

Ranzel surprised himself by laughing. He couldn't remember the last time he laughed.

Had he ever?

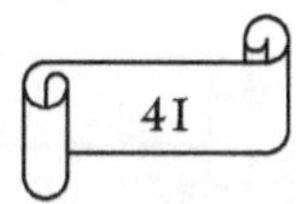

Knowing she'd pushed the mage far enough with words, Flynn decided to disarm Ranzel in a different way. "Let's see what your magic can do," Flynn said.

If Ranzel had known better, had known that a mischievous look in a strong woman's eye was reason to worry, he would have been much, much less likely to agree.

BECAUSE RANZEL REFUSED to leave the tower, they cleared a space in the tower level where they had met and Flynn had slept. It was like a great room garden with the creek flowing around the curve of the stone and disappearing through a hole in the floor. However, in the center of the room was that massive, beautiful rug and an excessive amount of expensive furniture.

Flynn moved all of this carefully aside as Ranzel watched in bemusement.

In no time, she had moved two large armchairs, a small table set, numerous books, and various potted plants. Then, she rolled up the massive rug and placed it near the grassy area surrounding the

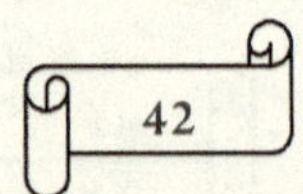

unnatural creek. Finally happy with the room, Flynn turned to Ranzel.

"Let's fight," she said.

"I do not understand," he responded.

"I will attack with superior fighting skill, and you will use your physical magic to defeat me."

"No," Ranzel said.

"Yes," Flynn said. "I've seen the books you read. All are about magic and developing your craft. Having spent your life in this tower, I'm sure you've never tested your magic in this way. Why not take the opportunity to develop your skill, your magical reach? As a soldier, I need to train and keep sharp. Otherwise, some crazy creature of this isle will finish me off, and then you'll be alone again. We need to fight, so you can become better and I can stay good."

Ranzel couldn't argue with that.

And so they fought.

Flynn won. Flynn was right, Ranzel had never tried to change his physicality in the way she suggested. He could shift, putting on a new look. It was like pulling on a different set of clothes. Easy. The magic he had done with Zelroth to bring the

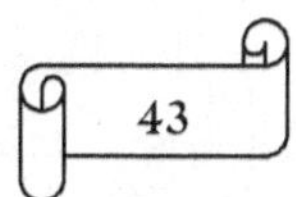

princes to negotiation was different. It had been a combination of his power over the physical, Zelroth's ability to control emotions, the blood of the princes, and other potions. Together, it had made a powerful tether which enabled a manipulation of the physical he didn't understand and couldn't duplicate on his own.

What Flynn was asking him to do now was to stretch himself—literally. And also to shrink. Reaching to land a blow, shrinking to dodge one. He managed tiny spurts of power, but they did little.

Sitting on an ice block he had gathered from the magical ice house below, Ranzel eyed Flynn. The girl was deceptively strong. And impressive.

Ranzel had *not* been impressive. Not at all. The thought left Ranzel displeased. Displeased he had been beaten so thoroughly by the soldier. Displeased he had been knocked on his backside so many times. Displeased he looked a fool sitting on a block of ice for comfort as the soldier moved about without a care.

Flynn *was* pleased. Pleased at finding a sparring partner, albeit an unwilling one, and pleased she had

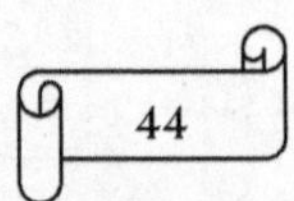

been following her plan. She'd been containing her curiosity, gleaning information rather than demanding it. It was difficult not to interrogate Ranzel, but he wasn't a prisoner.

Well, he wasn't her prisoner. He was the tower's prisoner.

But she had gotten some information about his magic and his personality. And sparring always built rapport, right? She turned to Ranzel, noting that though he appeared unhappy, he also seemed relaxed. "Who created this magical space?" she asked as she trailed a finger over a curling vine.

"Zelroth." Ranzel said, shifting uncomfortably on the ice.

"Who is Zelroth?" Ranzel froze, and Flynn backstepped, saying, "It's nice. I love the running water. This has everything you need to survive. But no adventure."

"Adventure is overrated," Ranzel said defensively. His most recent taste of adventure had been bitter. He and Zelroth had traveled for months acquiring the blood for the prince's tethers. It was the only time he'd left the tower in years. The world had

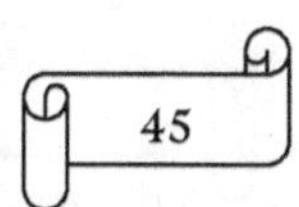

seemed so loud and so vast. Coupling that with the need for him to use his magic to get close to royal prince after royal prince and steal some of their blood had made the whole experience less than pleasant. It had been a questionable, nerve-wracking business. How relieved he had been when Zelroth told him he could return to the tower and didn't have to go to Athaleen, that he'd procured their prince's blood through other means.

Yes, staying here was so much better than leaving, yet…

"It gets boring," Ranzel said, looking sad. And as if his physical magic had spread to her, her face mimicked his, showing sadness too. For Flynn could think of nothing worse than a boring life. A life without anyone to please.

In the following days, Flynn soaked in the novelty of a quiet life. She stayed patient, gleaning information. She made it a game to appear as innocent and unsuspecting as possible. She channeled her sister's abilities: diplomatic, aloof, flirty, and friendly. At first, she struggled in her role, wanting all the answers now, but as the days went

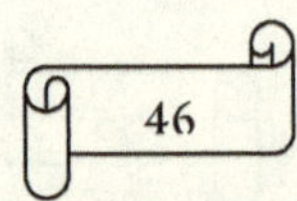

on, she felt less and less rushed. She stopped pretending to be at ease and became legitimately relaxed.

She explored the tower, finding many interesting things but little to aid in her understanding of her brothers' curse. On the bottom floor, she found a locked door. When she asked Ranzel about it, his face went ashen, then turned an unnatural blotchy red. He'd made her swear to never enter that room before refusing to discuss it ever again.

It was a part of the tower that felt different, separate from the rest of the enchanted stone and the reclusive mage. Ranzel never entered it, and after days of using every ability to please and cajole she possessed, she finally accepted its secrets would stay locked away.

But she hated the secrecy of that place.

Her favorite room of the tower was the top level. It was glass, all glass. Walls, ceiling, everything. She didn't know how the illusion made them look like stone from the outside, but she liked this vast room full of nature and space. Even more surprising, she liked the quiet man who lived there. He was quiet,

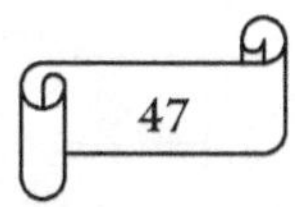

but the words he did share were kind, interesting, and showed a wisdom beyond his life experiences.

The princess made the mistake of getting comfortable. And a soldier should never be too comfortable.

# Chapter Five

FLYNN CHEERED. "You almost dodged that one! I'll make you a magic soldier yet!"

Stepping from her makeshift sparring ring, the soldier-princess ended their daily training. With dramatic heaves and woeful sighs, she replaced the massive rug and began tugging the heavy furnishings back into place.

Working beside her, Ranzel ignored her theatrical performance. This show of Flynn's was as much of a routine as the fighting. She figured if she complained enough, Ranzel would give in and leave the tower. Flynn tried almost every day to get him to leave, but he would never leave, so she never left.

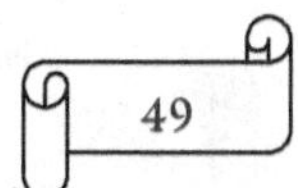

Sliding the last chair into place, she said, "You know, if we left the tower, we could not only avoid all this fuss of moving things around, but we would have more room to spar."

"The difficulty of entry and exit makes it a foolish endeavor," Ranzel justified.

"Well, I think a larger area would benefit your fighting style," Flynn argued.

Ranzel just grunted because his 'fighting style' was more of a try-to-survive-by-avoiding-the-crazed-soldier, and it lacked in every possible way. A larger area was only going to give him more space in which to lose. He most definitely didn't possess any type of form, discipline, or *style*.

Once the room was set to rights, Flynn crouched to drink from the creek. The water was the purest, best water she had ever tasted. She sighed in relief. The sparring kept her from getting antsy, calmed her need to know. She leaned back against the grass growing near the waterway. It was strange, the mixture of grass and stone, but the princess didn't mind. In these moments, she found enjoyment in this mission that was more vacation than adventure.

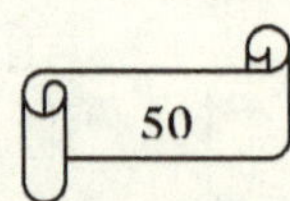

After quenching his thirst, Ranzel sat next to her on the grass. He rested on one arm and lazily skimmed his hand over the fresh water, thoughtful.

Flynn studied his face, trying to read his mood. Would he give her more information today? "What do you do?" she asked, her voice low and her words slow. "I mean, before I came and forced you to fight. What would you do every day?"

Ranzel shrugged. "I would read, study maps. Just the care of the tower takes time. The magic can't do it alone."

"So, the magic has limits," she said.

"Yes, I suppose all magic does. Magic doesn't think. It only does what it is directed or shaped to do. For example, if I didn't harvest from the garden, it would keep providing, growing out of control." His eyes took on the distant gaze of memories, and a soft smile spread across his face. "Once, I forgot to gather the ice from the bottom level. By the time I remembered, the stairway was full of melting ice. It had just kept on with its daily production, the new block shoving all the others aside. It was a long, cold afternoon carrying the blocks to dispose of them out

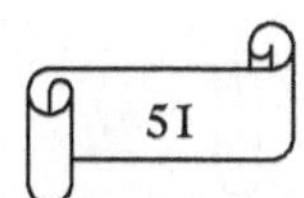

the window." Flynn held her breath, hoping his story would go on. He had never before shared so freely.

Ranzel's eyes kept that distant look, and he said, "The tower is spelled to provide all a person could need. Forever." He flicked the water from his hands and continued flicking his hands long after they were dry, his gaze on some future Flynn couldn't see. The water dried on the mage's hand, but still he flicked his fingers.

Slowly, Flynn reached over and touched his hand, stopping his absentminded movement. The two had touched before while sparring. Of course, they had. But this was different. Flynn found herself hesitant to end the contact.

Meeting Ranzel's expressive eyes, she saw his face soften. His look somehow familiar.

Finally, she pulled her hand away and rested it on the grass.

Ranzel laid his hand next to hers on the grass, his finger almost brushing against her own. He studied her small, elegant fingers closely. Without taking his focus from her hand, he said, "You're welcome to stay with me, Flynn. I'll tell Zelroth. I'm sure he'll

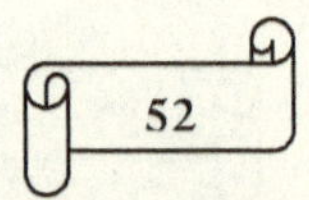

allow you to stay. Especially if I mention your aid in expanding my magic."

"Why must we have Zelroth's permission?" Flynn responded, her voice pitched low as she attempted to control her emotions. Ranzel was opening up to her finally, so there was excitement. This was an expected emotion. A welcome emotion. An emotion she felt during all of her adventures. That's what this excitement was. That was why she couldn't take her eyes from his hand so close to her own.

But she knew it was more than excitement. He was also offering her a boring, safe, limited life, and for a mere second, the idea held merit. It was appealing. To forsake everything for this tower. This secretive mage. His restricting, impossible idea made her feel…interested, intrigued. Tempted.

She shifted her hand into a fist, creating a distance between them, hoping his next words would give her clarity.

And his words did. They gave her far more clarity than she wanted.

"He's my master," Ranzel said with a shrug, like it was normal for a grown man to have a master. "The

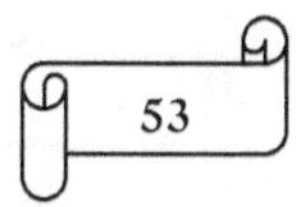

mage who took me under his wing and taught me all I know about magic. He brought me here for my safety and leaves me here for my protection. Until he can make the world a safe place for mages like me, I'll stay here."

"The Maker is the true master, Ranzel," Flynn practically whispered.

"That's not what Master Zelroth says," Ranzel said, standing in his agitation.

"It's what I say," Flynn said, refusing to raise her voice or to stand. "I believe the Maker is there to guide my life, to make me better. But it doesn't matter what I think or what Zelroth thinks. What matters is what you think."

Ranzel's defensiveness deflated, and he eased into a soft chair. He'd never been asked what he thought, and he was determined to actually do it. "I think," he finally answered, "I think Zelroth is real. And he will improve this world."

"How will he make the world safe?" Flynn asked as her stomach churned with foreboding.

"Oh, he was meeting with royalty and working on negotiations, but something went wrong. He had to

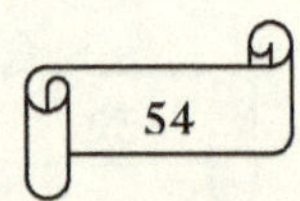

disappear. But he'll be back. He always comes back." Ranzel smiled at Flynn as if his words were reassuring.

Flynn suppressed the urge to look behind her for this mysterious mage. She had a sneaking suspicion this master would recognize her, a soldier of Athaleen. This mage, who told his apprentice he'd been *negotiating* with princes. Perhaps Ranzel knew exactly what these *negotiations* were. Flynn prayed he didn't. Because her brother and the other ten princes hadn't been negotiating, but were being tortured through deadly battles. And negotiations and mortal peril were two very, very different things. But Ranzel probably didn't know what was happening. He knew so little.

"Did he do these negotiations on this isle?" Flynn asked, her voice even more tight and more controlled than before.

"Yes, yes, he did. But a few months ago, things went wrong. Possible with the tether we had made for the princes. Hopefully, he's finding a resolution. Maybe he's meeting with them elsewhere. Perhaps I won't have to remain in this tower much longer."

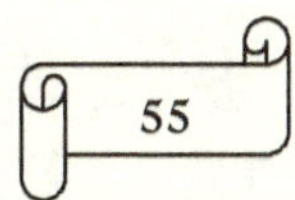

Ranzel beamed at the thought.

Flynn smiled back at him hollowly. Ranzel admitted it. He had been a part of the prince's curse. He had helped force the princes to fight magical creatures to the death night after night. Ranzel may have been innocent in some ways, but he was culpable in others. How could this be? How could she explain it to him? And why would he believe her truths over his master's lies?

Flynn rose and made some excuse about needing to polish her sword. Ranzel leaned back on the tower floor, blissfully unaware of the evil manipulations of his master.

Flynn stumbled down the stairs to the kitchen area, her throat closing with each step. Soon her breathing was tight, shallow. She found herself leaning over the hearth, gasping.

Panic. This was panic.

Why, she didn't know. She'd always suspected the tower, but she'd stopped suspecting Ranzel. She'd let herself grow attached. And so had he. With a start, she realized why the soft look he had given her there in the magical grass had seemed familiar. It was the look Humphrey often gave Tesha. The indulgent one. The heartfelt one. The lovesick one.

Flynn's panic increased, dropping her to her knees. He couldn't love her. He didn't know her. She was a fraud. And she couldn't love him. He was prisoner to a lifetime of lies. A mage who misused his magic.

Her vision grew fuzzy, her lungs as ineffective as her paralyzed and overwrought mind. There were so many emotions. So many unfamiliar and suffocating emotions.

She had gotten too comfortable here. She hadn't seen what should have been obvious. For the first time in her life, Flynn admitted that this adventure was beyond her abilities. No training had prepared her for this. She needed her home, not this poor substitute. But she also needed as much information as she could gather. She owed herself, her family, her kingdom, and her Maker the truth.

And Flynn knew exactly where to find it.

This decision helped Flynn slow her breathing. Her heart calmed and her mind cleared as she created a new plan. The wooden door. She needed to

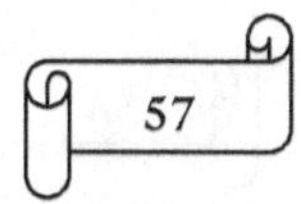

see what was in that secretive space. Flynn had been waiting, denying the itch to pick the lock in the hopes that Ranzel would relent, but she wasn't going to wait anymore.

Luckily, Ranzel was a creature of strict habits. Every afternoon, he climbed to the glass room and sat amongst the flowering blossoms there, meditating. Like much of the rest of his schedule, Flynn had been joining him, but not today. The princess was through settling into this twisted, tangled life.

Making her excuses, she crept down the stairs. Slipping the tiny tools she'd collected from various rooms in the tower from her pocket, she quickly picked the lock. The door swung open on loud, unused hinges, and she waited, listening for sounds from above.

All was silent and still. Everything. The mysteries beckoned, but the room itself was uninviting.

Flynn didn't hesitate. Grabbing a candle from another pocket, she lit it, slunk in, and closed the door behind her. Even with her weak candle in the misty darkness, it didn't take her long to discover the

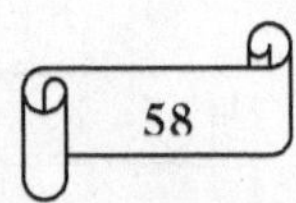

evidence she was equally hoping and dreading to find.

There in the basement were row upon row of full glass vials. The murky vapor was familiar to Flynn. She had seen it here on this island, this magic released from the princes as they strove to protect. It was power in a bottle. All of the power stripped from her brothers and the other cursed princes. Every night another battle, another vial, another theft for this arsenal of magical strength.

The rows and shelves seemed to expand before Flynn, going on forever. She paced down the long aisles, her horror growing.

How much magic was stored here? How much damage could be done with this power? Was it enough to take down a kingdom?

The thought made Flynn sick, and she lurched to one side, bumping into a metal grating. She lifted the candle for a better view and recognized a cage. A skeleton littered the floor. Flynn stumbled backward, even sicker than before.

In her haste, she bumped against the wall. With a creaky movement, a piece of the wall gave way.

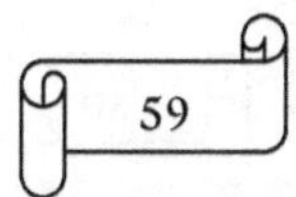

Without thought, Flynn darted for the opening, needing air. Needing to escape the tower and its horrible secrets.

Once she stepped free, she couldn't stop. She cleared the opening, hardly noticing the sound of the hidden door slamming shut behind her. She stumbled forward, then, raising her heels, she ran faster and faster and faster.

She couldn't stay a second longer in that tower. She needed to escape. Athaleen. Home. She needed to warn them.

The cliff stopped her headlong run. If it hadn't been there, she might have dashed straight into the sea and attempted to swim the dangerous channel.

Instead, she pulled up short, inches from the cliff's ledge. The sea churned below her, and she strained her eyes, scanning the waters, hoping for a familiar ship.

There were none to be found. Only the howl of a wind that echoed the howling inside. Still, she searched, scanning, praying to find a way back home. She so desperately needed and wanted help that she didn't notice how close she was to the edge.

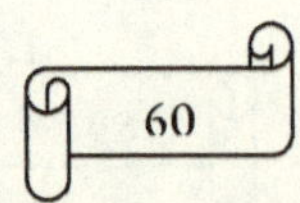

And when that angry, snapping wind struck again, Flynn tumbled toward the waters below.

# Chapter Six

*SURVIVE. SURVIVE. SURVIVE.*

That singular word pounded into Flynn's mind as she fell. In the tiny scrap of time before hitting the crashing waves, she gathered her feet beneath her and sucked in a sharp breath.

Then she was swallowed by the sea.

Surprisingly, the cold shocked her first, and for an instant, she just sank, unmoving. The violence of the waters shocked her next, compelling her to scramble to the surface.

She rose, gasped for air, and was pulled back under again. This cycle continued. On and on. With each resurfacing, she attempted to gain her bearings,

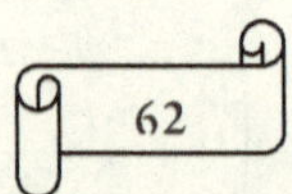

to find an escape. After more dunkings than she wished to experience in the entirety of her life, she saw it: a slip of sandy beach to her right.

Getting there meant swimming between a mass of protruding rocks and the cliff face. Staying in this more open section of the sea meant drowning. Two bad options. If she were lucky, she'd navigate the passageway without being dashed into the rocks.

Feeling rather *unlucky,* she pushed for the beach. The waves seemed to help her in her quest, happily pushing her toward the more dangerous section of the sea. *Maniacal waters,* she thought as her arms sliced through their freezing depths. She refused to take her eyes off the sand that promised survival. Even as the waves began frantically churning around her, pushing her everywhere but where she wanted to go, she kept her gaze fastened on the shore.

*Survive. Survive.*

Flynn pressed on. The waves threw her leg into a rock. She felt a terrible pain at her ankle, but she pressed on. Her torso was slammed against the cliff, leaving her whole left side burning despite the cold. She pressed on. She was almost free when the waters,

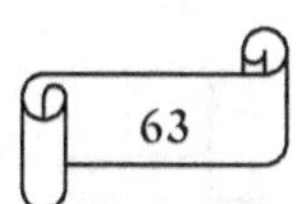

with one last effort to end her, pulled her under and smashed her head into a waiting rock.

She felt the blackness creeping in, the ominous recession of all her pain. *Press on. Survive.* She forced the conviction to fill her mind, pushing the darkness back.

And then she was there, the sand shifting under her grasping hands. The waves pushed and lapped at her legs as if commending her for winning their battle and asking her to play again. She kicked and clawed her way up the beach away from those horrible waters.

She collapsed on the damp shore. She'd survived.

But the wind wanted to play, too. It drove at her, freezing her chilled body and throwing grit into her wounds. The soldier-princess closed her eyes against the attack, analyzing her weaknesses and preparing her counter-attack.

Her ankle was badly damaged, possibly broken. Her other side was cut to pieces, stinging and bleeding. Her head was the most concerning. A hazy darkness was hovering at the corner of her vision, and blood was dripping down her temple.

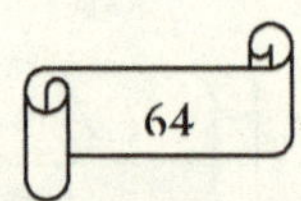

Another darkness threatened as well, the darkness of night. Flynn needed to get back to the tower, she'd hoped to never return to. She needed Ranzel.

With faltering, clumsy movements, she ripped away a sleeve from her tattered shirt and bandaged her head. Ignoring the wind whipping at her clothes, she tightened the laces on her soaked boots, grimacing at the pressure on her wounded ankle. Her side she ignored, the cold too concerning.

Prepared for this new battle, she stood.

The wind spiraled around her, gleeful. It was the brutal wind's turn to see if it could break this princess, if it could finish the job the waves had started.

*Survive.* Flynn braced herself before throwing her body at this new foe. With a powerful rush up the steep bank, she made her way back onto the cliff where the battle had begun.

*Survive.*

RANZEL WAS ANGRY. He had been confused. Then concerned. Then sad.

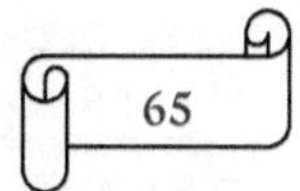

But now he was raging, pacing the length of his tower again and again.

She had unlocked the door! She'd entered Master Zelroth's private sanctuary. Without a word to him. And after he had asked her to stay! He had offered her a place in his tower to live in safety, and she had betrayed him and left! Worse, she had left without a word. It was cowardly. Unlike the soldier he thought he knew.

She must have been planning to betray him all along. She'd had a plan. To learn about Zelroth and leave. She had used him. Why else would she leave the tower? The isle was dangerous, and here it was safe. At least it had been. What if she brought her army back? Would his tower be safe then?

No, Flynn had ruined everything. He should never have let her in. He paced a rather vigorous circuit around the large living space. The wind pummeled against the tower, pushing through the window and leaving the room in disarray. Another gust followed, and he rushed to close the shutters against it.

That's when he saw her.

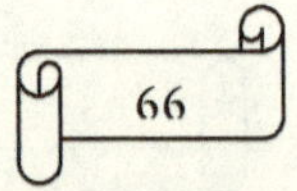

His anger disappeared in an instant. She was injured. She faltered, falling to her knees. He stood at the window, frozen in disbelief and indecision. He needed to go to her. He couldn't leave. She needed him. He had given a vow.

The pitiful figure of Flynn was still some distance from his tower across a vast meadow. There she began crawling, covering the last hundred yards on her knees. Not knowing of the hidden door, Ranzel believed she wouldn't be able to climb to him, but if he went down to her, they would both be stuck outside the tower.

He could see her shivering from his perch in the tower. He knew she needed warmth and healing. She needed him.

Revitalized, he did what he did best. What he had spent a lifetime studying to do.

He used his magic to create just what she needed.

By the time Flynn collapsed at the base of the tower, he was ready. His magical rope dropped down to her, fashioned with a large loop for her to sit in as he hefted her to safety. He hoped she had the strength to hold on. Somehow, she had held on to her life for this long, and he chose to trust in her waning strength.

Flynn just stared at the rope in shock.

Ranzel almost climbed down to assist her, though the return trip would be difficult. Then the soldier moved, sliding the rope over her head, around her waist, and under her legs. With a grimace, she clung to the rope.

Ranzel began pulling.

By the time Flynn cleared the opening, she was barely clinging to consciousness, much less the rope. Ranzel had to grab her and heft her to the floor. She fell unceremoniously on top of him.

"Survive," she murmured, her face pressed against his tunic. "Survive."

"Yes, Flynn," he said, sparing a second to press her to him, "you will survive."

Determined, Ranzel shimmied free, lifted her in his arms, and placed her near the fire. He quickly decided her head was the worst injury. Placing his hand on the bloody bandage, he braced himself. Then, he magically syphoned her pain. The intensity of it sent him reeling, and he barely maintained

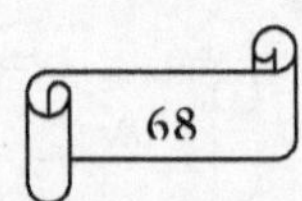

enough coherence to tap into his magic and heal the wound. Next, he took the pain from her side. Then her ankle.

Having already used so much magic on the rope, the collective effort of taking her pain and healing it was exhausting.

He collapsed on the ground next to her. She was healed, but still so, so cold. And so, he reached out a hand, touched her cheek, and pulled the penetrating cold from her trembling frame to his exhausted one.

He lost consciousness before he could heal it. Instead, the towered mage and the fighting princess lay on the stone floor. But they didn't lie dying.

No, they were surviving.

# Chapter Seven

FLYNN STIRRED FIRST. With her eyes closed, she timidly stretched, expecting to feel pain. When she found none, her eyes sprang open.

She was almost relieved to see the tower's stone ceiling. For a moment, she had thought the tower, Ranzel, and the perilous swim had all been a dream, and she would wake back in her royal suite at home. Home. She wanted to go home, but Ranzel needed her.

And she needed him.

She had known he would save her. The second she cleared the embankment, she knew all she had to do was get to the tower, to Ranzel. Somehow, he would

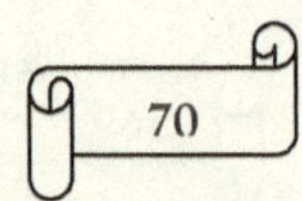

save her. Well, that and her determination to get back to him, her faith that his magic would be enough.

Usually, Flynn hated needing things from other people. She was a giver, not a taker. She'd learned at a young age to value pleasing others and was very successful at doing so. She had begrudgingly learned to support and be supported in the army, but she didn't like making demands. She liked to be the helper, the one offering aid.

Odd that it didn't bother her to need Ranzel. It felt more freeing, somehow, to have his support.

Ranzel was...important. He was good and strong and sweet. He was...sleeping next to her with his arm draped across her waist.

Flynn's musings ground to a halt.

With a quick, smooth movement, she shifted her body until she was facing him fully. Ranzel stirred, his arm tightening its hold, but he didn't waken.

He wasn't striking. He was perfectly average. A slow, tender smile spread across her face as she scanned his attractive features. How like him to be so notable while wishing to be nondescript. As the morning light stretched across the room, the last of

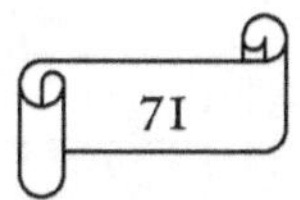

her anger at him slipped away. He wasn't her enemy. He wasn't evil. Regardless of her feelings, she owed him the knowledge of what this tower really was. If she had left, if a ship had magically turned up on that shore, she would have hated herself for leaving him here. A victim. He was her responsibility. No, he was simply hers.

There was so much Ranzel needed to know. Knowledge that would complicate everything. She was a *princess*. And Ranzel didn't seem to have too high an opinion of royalty.

Flynn's smile faded as she considered the secrets between them. But there was a truth Ranzel needed to face before her own. He needed to know of the secret room and the princes' curse. He needed to know what his master had done, was doing. He needed to understand what he had unwittingly been a part of.

He deserved her help. He deserved so much more than the life Zelroth had forced him to accept. He deserved the truth.

Everything hinged on how he reacted to that knowledge.

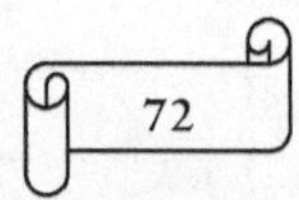

Because Ranzel was a responsibility, but so was Athaleen. Her kingdom and family needed the information she had, and if Ranzel tried to get in the way of that mission….

Flynn shut off her dark thoughts, focusing on the priorities. When Ranzel woke, they would talk. She still needed answers, but Ranzel did, too. Only, he wasn't asking questions—he'd spent a lifetime avoiding certain truths. But if faced with the truth, he would have to choose. And Flynn would get him to see the truth.

With a heavy heart, Flynn slipped from under Ranzel's arm and gained her feet. She bounced quietly up and down on her toes, testing her ankle, rubbing a hand down her once-injured side, and shaking her healed head.

Physically, she felt amazing. Mentally and emotionally, she was a twisted mess.

To calm her mind, she focused on the tangible. The fire was still burning in the hearth. She added a few logs. Her footwear was still damp. She removed her boots, tilting toward the heat to speed up the drying process. She pulled the bandage from her

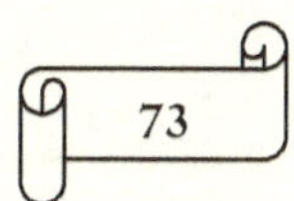

head. A wave of gratitude crashed over her as she held the bloody fabric in her hands, and she dropped to her knees, praying in thanks.

Rising, she tossed the stained bandage into the fire and turned to survey the room. It was clean and organized except for a rope coiled haphazardly next to the window. She went to it, curious.

Flynn had previously searched the tower for rope. She had hoped to find an easier way to leave the tower than down-climbing. She had even asked Ranzel for one, but he had claimed there were none. He didn't need one because he never needed to leave his magical tower.

Crouching, Flynn picked up the braided rope. It was made of an interesting material. It almost looked like—

"It's hair."

Starting at Ranzel's voice or maybe the fact that the rope was made of *hair,* Flynn threw the rope down and jumped away.

"Yours?" Flynn asked. Both a little disgusted and impressed by the creation, her voice was filled with awe.

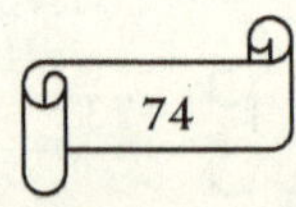

"Yes," Ranzel said, gaining his feet. Then, grinning at Flynn, he concentrated his power. His hair grew an inch and then another.

Flynn shot forward, grabbing his now shoulder-length hair. "Your magic is amazing! Healing and regenerative powers. How great is that!" Giving his hair a tug here and there, she combed her fingers through the choppy strands. "That's amazing," she said, flitting around Ranzel.

When she moved back in front of him, he stopped her with a light touch to her waist. He studied her eyes closely, then stepped back to evaluate the rest of her welfare. "Are you well?" he asked, his gaze seemed to unlock a new ability in Flynn's heart. The ability to flutter and pound and dance all at the same time. Knowing now wasn't the time to focus on this new and interesting ability, Flynn laid her hands atop Ranzel's and eased it from her waist.

She kept her hold of his hand, clinging tightly to it. Pausing, she reached for his other hand. She looked from their clasped hands to his penetrating gaze and said, "I'm perfectly well, thanks to you, your magic hair, and your healing. Unfortunately, this isle isn't

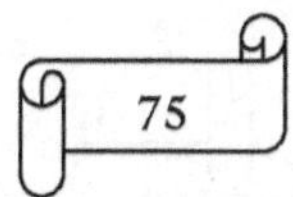

well. This tower isn't what you have been led to believe. And after what I must show you, I fear *you* will not be well for some time."

"What—" Ranzel wasn't sure what he had expected from Flynn. An explanation as to why she ran off and how she'd gotten hurt? A celebratory sparring session? A show of affection? An apology? Instead, she was dismantling his life, his home, his very existence.

"There's something I must show you," she said, her musical voice more somber than he had ever heard it.

"Where?" Ranzel said, looking about the tower as if this horrible thing was right in front of his eyes. And a horrible thing *had* been right in front of his eyes all along, or at least beneath his feet.

"The locked room—"

"You should have never—"

"I know, I shouldn't have promised I wouldn't search it. I knew I would have to eventually." Ranzel jerked his hands from hers, but Flynn continued, "I am a soldier, Ranzel. I have to protect Athaleen, and this isle has threatened and continues to threaten my

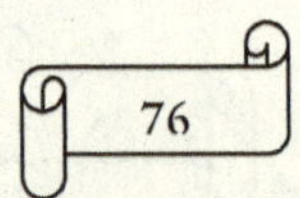

home." She stepped closer to him, waiting until he met her eyes. When he did, they were full of confusion and despair. She forced herself to say, "You need to see the potion room," but Flynn doubted the potion room would be enough to convince Ranzel of Zelroth's lies. She wasn't even sure she could explain or demonstrate the power in those potions, having no idea of the potency. Besides, he deserved to see all and make a choice of his own.

And so, Flynn looked Ranzel right in the face, clasped his shoulders, prayed he would agree, believed he would see the necessity, and hoped he would trust her as she said, "We have to leave the tower."

THE ARENA was just as she had left it. A large circular stone structure with stairs up one side. She guided Ranzel up these stairs, darting up them and back down as he followed at a careful, leery pace.

Flynn hadn't realized the toll leaving the tower would take on Ranzel, but as they dropped from the tower window and into the openness of the isle, he

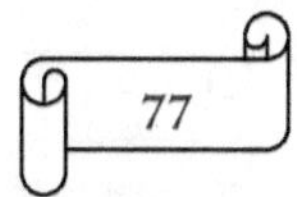

had grown paler and paler. His face had pinched, his eyes darted frantically around, and his body coiled as if prepared to flee back to the safety of the tower.

Flynn wasn't sure if the anxiety was caused by what he had seen in the potion room or not. Ranzel had taken in the room with one quick sweep, but refused to step inside, mumbling something about too many promises broken. Which is why they'd been forced to exit via the rope.

The entire trip, Ranzel stayed quiet, withdrawn. To compensate, Flynn skipped around him, chattering about adventures she'd been on with her troop while she led him through the more open areas, avoiding the heavily forested spaces. He had yet to relax, and Flynn was beginning to despair of him when they reached the top of the arena.

Exercising a self-control she was beginning to loathe, Flynn quieted. Waiting to see Ranzel's reaction, she stepped back and gave him space to explore. He inched forward.

Body taunt, he moved to the edge of the wall, staring down into the arena. His brow pinched, and he whirled to the lone stone bench at the top of the

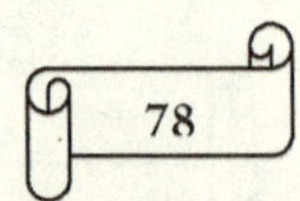

tower before eying the walkway all along the rim. With careful steps, he avoided a small pile of glass shards and picked up a shattered vial. Then another.

He held the strings up to the light. "Do you recognize those?" Flynn whispered.

Ranzel nodded. "They're the remains of the tethers Zelroth wore to summon the princes."

Confusion deepened in the lines of his brow as he searched for access down into the arena, but there were no stairs. He stared across the arena, where there was a large, metal portcullis gate. It was partially raised, the bottom row of its spiked grating suspended in the air. This was the only exit to be seen, meaning once a person was in, they couldn't get out unless let out.

The arena was a trap. Ranzel saw it. The empty cages, the old carcasses of monsters on the arena floor.

"What is this place?" he whispered in horror.

Flynn sat on the stone bench and patted the small space next to her. With drooping shoulders and a restlessly tapping foot, she watched him approach. She knew this conversation would be awful.

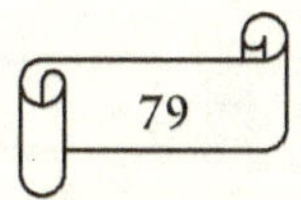

Ranzel would believe her and be hurt. *Or* he would think she was lying and be hurt. Either way would hurt.

Taking a deep breath, Flynn said, "This is where Zelroth had his negotiations."

# Chapter Eight

RANZEL SAT ON THE STONE BENCH at the top of the arena. Sitting probably wasn't the right word; with his features fixed in a solemn expression and his body unmoving, he looked more like he was merging with the stone. A part of him wished he could.

Flynn had left to wander around the lower level of the arena, wisely giving Ranzel space to process the truth of Zelroth and the arena. More significantly, to grapple with his personal involvement in the curse. Dismay. Guilt. Betrayal. He was coping with it all. He felt frozen, unwilling and unmotivated to move. They would be lucky to make it back to the tower before dark.

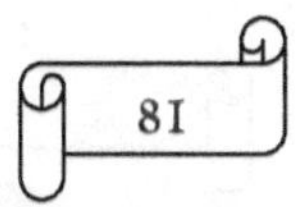

*At least I have her…for now.* With that darkly optimistic thought, Ranzel watched Flynn enter the arena, ducking under the partially raised portcullis. Weighed down under the heaviness of the day, she kicked at the soft dirt. It puffed up in clouds around her feet before settling again over the remnants of the previous battle.

Most of the monsters' carcasses had been carried away by the wild animals roaming the isle or picked clean by scavengers. Here and there, Ranzel saw a few fresh tracks, indicating some animals still used this as a hunting ground for an easy meal. If an animal came to scavenge, they would be trapped with only one exit. Easy prey.

Ranzel's gaze grew distant as Flynn moved further and further from the gate. He believed her tale, had all the proof he could ever need before him and a wealth of questionable memories of his master.

When he was younger, Zelroth had spouted hateful rhetoric about royalty and how he would make them pay. The more Ranzel questioned the need for such violent methods, the more mellow Zelroth became in his ideology. At least that's what

Ranzel had believed, but in truth, he had been blinding his apprentice to his true plans. He had been using Ranzel's magic in evil ways and convincing him it was all in the name of unity, peace, and acceptance.

By hiding in the tower, Ranzel had allowed himself to be led astray. He had trusted blindly, had let fear keep him hidden, had not lived by his own conviction. But never again.

Flynn crouched, retrieving an abused dagger buried in the sand. Ranzel almost smiled watching her toss it from one hand to the next and jab it at an imaginary foe. The soldier's hopeful optimism, her engaging presence, was *that* powerful—strong enough to force Ranzel to consider joy in a moment like this.

Suddenly, Flynn froze, her hand tightening around the dagger. She shifted in the sand, spinning in a slow, cautious half-circle. From an open cage came a snarl, two yellow eyes, and a large paw.

Snapping from her stillness, Flynn jammed the dagger into her belt, pulled her bow free, snatched an arrow from her quiver, strung the bow, and fired.

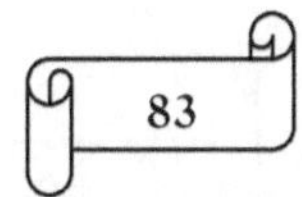

The cat sprang from the cage. With an arrow embedded high in its shoulder, it charged angrily at Flynn. She got one more shot off before it lunged. As soon as the cat was airborne, Flynn dove under it, rolling across in the dirt.

The beast spun around, and Flynn pulled the dagger free from her belt. The two enemies circled each other, two steps one direction, two steps the other.

Deciding it was through playing with its food, the cat launched itself at Flynn. She rushed to meet it, but before they could connect, the cat was knocked to the ground by a force from above.

Ranzel.

Deciding she would berate him later, Flynn took advantage of the distraction and finished the poor beast off with a skilled knife attack. The beast died with style, his legs stretched out beneath him, and his fangs bared.

Flynn skirted around the creature and advanced on Ranzel. "You shouldn't have done that!" she scolded, shoving his shoulders so forcefully he fell back a step. He barely registered her battery, his eyes

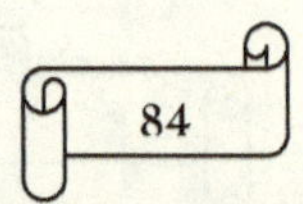

staring at the massive beast. Flynn changed tactics, "But you were amazing. What a leaping dive."

With numb, halting movements, Ranzel reached for the soldier, encircling her in his arms. "He made them fight that and worse, every night," he murmured. "Every single night." His arms tightened incrementally around Flynn until, eventually, she was pulled from her feet. Flynn didn't seem to mind. Instead, she clung to him just as tightly as he clung to her. He sighed into her intricately braided hair, soaking in the connection. The comfort.

After a time, Ranzel set her on her feet. "Let's go home," Flynn said, linking an arm through Ranzel's. It wasn't until much later that he realized what she had said.

Home. She'd called the tower home.

"WHAT HAPPENED AFTER YOU BROKE THE TETHERS?" Ranzel asked. His quiet voice filled the night air. They were lying in opposite directions, gazing at the darkened sky through the tower's enchanted ceiling.

Flynn had found him here, in the glass room of the tower, staring into the blackness. Half of the space was filled with a garden, and the loamy scent of plants and dirt comforted him. The other half of this space was his room, a simple bed and nightstand. Zelroth's room was here as well—again, a simple bed and nightstand. His true space was the potion room. That horrible space.

Next to him, Flynn shifted uncomfortably. It wasn't the ground causing her discomfort—a layer of ground cover cushioned their bodies—but his question. Ranzel assumed she was as uncomfortable with her history of the isle as he was. When she spoke, her voice was low, and she kept her eyes on the stars. "Captain Dalton broke eleven of the tethers, but in the struggle, she and Zelroth fell into the water. He escaped. In the arena, it was chaos. A prince and beast battle. Eventually, all of the tethers were broken, the princes set free, and the beasts killed. Then, some of the royalty took magic teleportation potions to get home. Everyone else took Zelroth's ship. They were escorted to their separate kingdoms with whatever assurances and knowledge we could give them. It wasn't much. But after all of the princes were safe, Athaleen made plans to come back to explore the isle. And that is how I came to be here again..."

Flynn finally slowed down in her diatribe before fading off in thought. She picked at her fingernails and slumped inward as culpability pressed down on her small frame. Her voice was small with shame when she spoke again, "There's something I haven't told you. Those teleportation—"

"Stop," Ranzel demanded, and Flynn froze in shock. Ranzel never demanded.

"Tell me another time, Flynn," he said, softening his voice. "I just want to process..."

"Absolutely," Flynn said, her voice thick with relief. After a moment, she asked with a smile. "Processing in silence? Or talking it out?"

Ranzel exhaled with a loud gust. "I suppose I should talk. I feel like a pawn. Foolish. I did everything to please Master Zelroth."

Flynn knitted her fingers together, resting them across her body. "It's not foolish to want to please. I do too. I want to please everyone. All the time. It gets

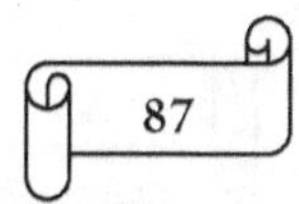

exhausting, but I don't think it's necessarily bad. If they're worthy of being pleased…"

"Am I?" Ranzel asked, unable to help himself.

"No, I mean, yes. I…"

Ranzel's emotions coiled and recoiled at her confusing words.

Flynn blew out a gusty breath, gathering her thoughts. When she did start speaking again, she did so with hands waving in the air. "You are worthy of being pleased, but I don't feel compelled to do so. It doesn't feel expected. I don't have to be what you need, I can just…be."

Her hands flopped back down onto her stomach, and she whispered. "It's nice."

Ranzel's lips curved, but he didn't respond, instead letting a peaceful quiet fill the room.

The stars moved across the sky for a time before he admitted, "I don't know what's next. If not the tower. Then where?"

"Athaleen accepts mages," Flynn suggested, then, before Ranzel could make a commitment he wasn't ready for, she continued, "I do have a question. About Zelroth. How does his magic work?"

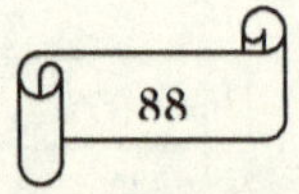

"I used to think he had magic of his own, but the more I think on it, I don't believe he does. He has used magic to control the emotions of people, but only through potions or artifacts like the tether. Which leads me to believe he syphoned it from someone. Like he syphoned physical magic from me. His is an amazing ability to create potions. To trap and manipulate the magic—and actions—of others."

"A mastermind," Flynn mumbled ruefully. "So, what will we do?"

Ranzel refused to embrace the warmth racing through him at her *we*, just as he refused to accept that this tower was her home.

Flynn had a kingdom. A light to share with so many.

"Do you want to confront him?" Flynn asked, wondering at the effectiveness of such a strategy. Ranzel was getting to be a better fighter, and she was a *great* one. If only they could find a way to disarm Zelroth of all magical potions…

Ranzel rose to rest his elbow on the ground. Facing Flynn, he said, "I want to understand him, to hear his side of the story."

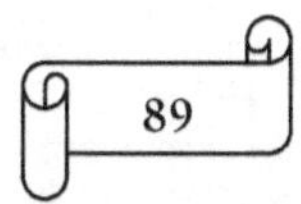

"His version!" Flynn sat up so quickly the blood rushed to her head, and she wobbled slightly. Ranzel reached to steady her, but she didn't notice. "Ranzel, what if he *can* magically manipulate your emotions? What if he uses a potion on you? He's shown what little value he has for life. For the royalty of the kingdoms. He deserves to pay for that. He is *evil.*"

Ranzel brushed his hand across the flowers beneath him and answered in a quiet voice. "He would say the same about them, Flynn. He deserves to be heard."

"No, he deserves to be punished." Flynn slammed her fist down, but the effect was greatly diminished by the cushioned surface.

Ranzel just shrugged. "I won't leave with you, Flynn. When your people come to find you, you need to go to warn Athaleen and the other kingdoms. But I'll be staying here."

Flynn tried to re-engage him, but soon realized he wouldn't be moved. He wouldn't be convinced.

He wouldn't go with her, but how could she leave him?

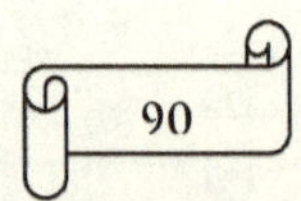

# Chapter Nine

FLYNN *WANTED* TO LEAVE THE ISLE. She really did. But she also wanted to stay.

If the winds cooperated, maybe a ship would come soon. She'd be home and back in weeks, likely before Zelroth returned. But the trade winds did *not* cooperate and every day they seemed to taunt her with their gusts. They danced around her ears, seeming to say, "Zelroth. Zelroth." The odds of her being gone when the master returned increased daily. The sooner she left, the sooner she could return. And the sooner she returned, the sooner Ranzel could know everything about her and she everything about him.

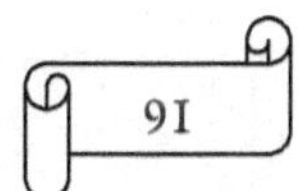

The princess-soldier searched the horizon for signs of a sail. The wind whipped at her, but with a healthy respect, she stood away from the cliff's edge. Ranzel stood behind her, refusing to let her *venture to that deadly cliff* alone.

Last night, she and Ranzel had made a sort of unspoken truce. She accepted he wasn't ready to wish death and destruction on his master and needed closure. And he accepted that she wanted justice and needed all the information she could get on the threat to her kingdom. Ranzel had given Flynn as much information on Zelroth as he could last night, but after years of manipulation, he wasn't sure what was true and what wasn't.

Flynn needed more information, and she knew where to find it. But not only was the wind making it difficult for her to act, but fear. Flynn feared that horrible place, but she needed to go in there. She needed to be the brave soldier she'd been trained to be. She needed to enter the potion room.

She turned from the cliff to find Ranzel smirking at her as the wind blew her hair in wild disarray about her head.

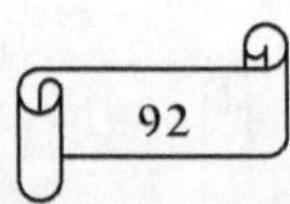

"You could just cut it off," he said after she voiced her displeasure.

"No, thank you," Flynn said, stuffing her long hair into her hood. "Not all of us can grow our hair back magically, and it's the one thing that makes me look like a p… like a powerful woman." She'd almost said princess. She needed to tell Ranzel, but now wasn't the time. And until she knew exactly where his loyalties lay, she should probably keep her royalty a secret. Probably. Maybe.

Her indecision and the danger of her heritage were just another reason to get off the isle.

Yes, she could wait. But she didn't *want* to. She wanted an army on the isle, waiting to take Zelroth. She wanted a life away from this isle, for both her and Ranzel.

"A powerful woman, huh?" Ranzel said, drawing her from her frustrated musings. Determined to make her smile, he continued, "The bow skills, those stunningly arresting eyes. They don't make you feel powerful enough?"

Flynn preened a bit at his words, straightening her shoulders and freeing her bow. "You aren't wrong,

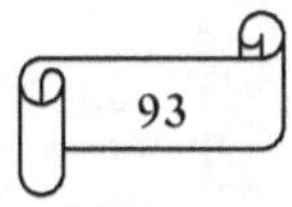

my friend. Those things are all defining parts, perhaps even the very essence, of a powerful woman. But my hair…," she shrugged her shoulders and skipped a step or two. "I guess I'm just vain."

"Is it vanity if there's cause?" Ranzel said as he fell into step beside her.

Flynn smirked, grateful for Ranzel's lightness, and said, "Oh, absolutely. That's the essence of vanity. Feeling vanity without cause just makes you foolish."

Ranzel laughed, entirely at ease. It was amazing how much freer the truth made him feel. But not entirely free, not yet. But he had hope—another thing he hadn't realized he was missing until he found it.

Back at the tower, Ranzel and Flynn practiced their fighting. Ranzel's ability to manipulate his physical appearance was growing. Making his hair, fingers, and even nose grow was easy. But making his arms or legs extend was much more difficult. His torso almost impossible.

The only way he had found to defeat Flynn was to do something ridiculous with his nose or hair and knock her down while she was laughing. It wasn't sporting, but Flynn didn't mind.

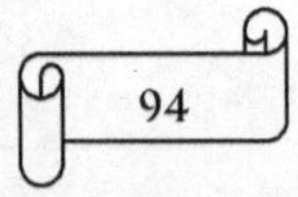

Still laughing from his latest extremely beak-like nose, Flynn collapsed next to the stream. She stretched out her legs and leaned back on her hands, forcing herself to relax. Her mirth fading, she studied Ranzel as he quenched his thirst.

"I wish you would come with me," she said in a low, compelling voice.

"As do I," he said, unwilling to even consider leaving without facing Zelroth.

"What if he never comes back?" Flynn asked.

"If what you said about the potion room is true, he will."

"Yes, the potion room…" she said in a soft voice. "I need to search it, Ranzel."

"I wish you wouldn't." Ranzel didn't say more, and he wouldn't get in her way. He'd explained his vow to Zelroth, and his determination to keep it. Even if Zelroth wasn't honest, he wanted to be. Flynn accepted this, but it created a distance.

A distance which grew into an unusual quiet and remained throughout the day. Finally, the awkwardness drove them apart—Ranzel to his room in the garden level and Flynn to her comfortable bed

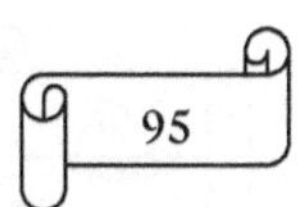

near the fire. But the princess didn't stay there long. Seeing no reason to put off the necessary task, she armed herself with her bow for security's sake and made her way down to the locked door. She made quick work of the lock and, ignoring the creaking hinge, made her way inside.

There, she lit her torch (much better for snooping around in dark places than a candle) and started exploring the shelves. Most of the room was filled with row upon row of the potion bottles. In the firelight, they shone a bright yellow color. There was also a vast number of colored bottles on a curving shelf, ingredients for potion making, and a massive wooden workspace pushed up against the tower wall.

Flynn avoided looking too closely into the metal cages and made her way to the bookcase. There, she packed interesting, forbidden-looking books into a bag, sparing only a moment to browse through their pages. She found a paper sitting on the corner of the desk, dusty from misuse but written on high-quality parchment.

Blowing off the dust, she read:

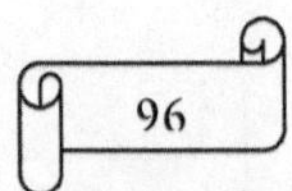

*Master Zelroth,*

*We are pleased to welcome you as the newest member of our society. The Sentinels value the talents not only of yourself, but of your young charge. Both of these skills will be much needed as we work to further the cause of The Sentinels. For your first assignment, please meet with your known contact in Athaleen. He will have more information on your first assignment. Again, welcome to our society. May magic reign forever.*

*The Sentinels*

The letter shook in Flynn's hand as she wondered just how many horrible secrets one room could hold. An agent in Athaleen? It was unthinkable. It was terrifying. It could arguably be the worst thing she'd seen on this isle: this proof that her own home wasn't safe.

The door scraped, opening further. Flynn turned to tell Ranzel, to show him this proof. But it wasn't Ranzel standing in the doorway, a torch highlighting his snarling face.

It was Master Zelroth. The mage had returned.

Now, *this*. This was the worst thing she'd ever seen.

Flynn attempted to pull her bow, but before she could even notch an arrow, a potion was thrown at her feet and darkness swarmed in.

# Chapter Ten

THE RISING AND FALLING cadence of two voices woke Flynn. They were too far away to make out individual words. All she heard was a quieter voice and a louder timber.

Ranzel and Zelroth.

What could they be speaking of? Was Ranzel confronting him? Had Zelroth discovered she had been living in the tower? Was Ranzel in trouble?

Locked in the dark back corner of the room, she could see very little. Her worries kept her company. They were terrible company, lingering where they weren't wanted. Flynn pushed them aside and focused on the voices. She remained still, straining to

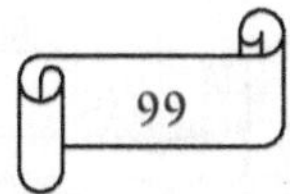

hear what was being said. The voices were so muffled, they must have been outside the room.

The master sounded frustrated, but not too angry. Ranzel sounded as Ranzel always sounded: calm, thoughtful. Suddenly, the door screeched open, and the words were clear.

"How could you not be aware of an intruder in the tower?" Zelroth demanded, looming in the doorway.

Ranzel's voice sounded from the hallway. "I was sleeping in my room. How would they get in?" Ranzel allowed fear to creep into his words. "Are we in danger? Is the tower failing?"

It seemed Zelroth had inadvertently taught Ranzel to manipulate. To act. And it was working. Zelroth wasn't suspicious. The master remained in the doorway, his tall form blocking the room, and addressed his apprentice. "Soon, young one," he said. "A big change is in motion."

"What happened with the negotiations?" Ranzel asked.

"They failed," Zelroth responded. "The young ones we hoped and worked so hard to influence are

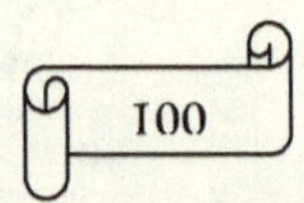

following in the footsteps of their fathers. Things are getting worse for us magic users, much worse. They are seeking out the babes with abilities. Selling them to foreign countries, or worse."

Zelroth leaned against the large wooden door and dropped his voice so low that Flynn could barely hear. "Athaleen is at the heart of the problem. This intruder is a soldier from Athaleen." He practically spat out the country's name, his voice thick with loathing. "I recognized her, she was here those months ago. She had a part in ruining the negotiations, in turning the princes against me."

"Perhaps we should set her loose on the sea," Ranzel said, and Flynn almost growled in offense. Ranzel continued, "Let the trade winds take her."

"That's it, my boy!" Zelroth said and slapped a hand on the cold, stone wall. "There's the passion our cause needs. But I don't have time for her at the moment. She can last a time in her cell, and if she can't. She can't."

"You have a cell in there?"

Ranzel infused his voice with enthusiasm, but Flynn could hear the underlying horror.

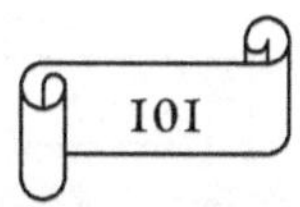

"Oh, young one," Zelroth said. "Sometimes I forget how little you know! It was a cage for animals, but it will work for her."

"I'd like to know more," Ranzel responded. Flynn mentally applauded his strategy. The best way for Ranzel to discover the truth was to be invited to participate more fully. Wisely, he told Zelroth, "I'd like to be able to assist. To further the cause. When the princes were coming for negotiations, it was amazing, knowing I was helping you night after night."

Zelroth didn't immediately respond. Flynn found herself holding her breath, and not just because the stench in her corner of the tower was awful. She waited, wondering if Zelroth would finally tell all. Or would he continue in his lies?

"Yes," Zelroth said, thoughtfully. "It is probably time you see what I have in storage and learn of our contingency plan. Actually what we have in store. I am a member of a group of like-minded mages. The Sentinels cause is ours, bringing mages and magic back to glory." The mage swung the door wide, and a beam of light fell on Flynn's cell. Flynn shied away

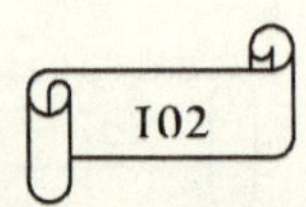

from it, hiding in the darkness, hoping Zelroth would forget all about her and keep talking.

He did, saying, "The negotiations with the princes were not fruitless. As I saw negotiations turning, I used my magic to quietly syphon off a bit of their power every night. These vials are all of that stored power."

As usual, Zelroth told a small part of the truth and hid a myriad of lies. He had been practicing this method for years, had perfected the art of manipulating Ranzel to get what he needed from him, but never giving back.

"But there are so many," Ranzel mused, his footsteps bringing him slowly closer to Flynn's cage.

"It was a tedious, but important work," Zelroth said, his tenor voice pitched with pride. "I would only syphon small, unnoticeable amounts from the royals. But they are so powerful, they never knew. So powerful," he said and drew a hand over a bright, yellow vial, "yet they do so little."

"Unlike The Sentinels," Ranzel said. He had avoided looking in Flynn's direction, but she'd seen his eyes darting her way. He probably wanted

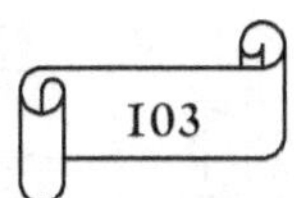

reassurance she was still okay, but so far, he'd gotten nothing.

Zelroth moved away from the cell, toward the door. "Yes, now that we know the isle isn't safe, the vials will need to be moved. I traveled by magic this time. In a few weeks, when the trade winds change, I will bring a ship. Then we sail to Athaleen."

"Athaleen?" Ranzel questioned. Flynn felt a horrible sinking pit in her stomach as Ranzel trailed after Zelroth. "Why Athaleen?" Ranzel said, asking the question she desperately needed answered.

"You shall see, young one," Zelroth said, exiting the potion room. "Now let us eat."

As he closed the door, Ranzel threw one last furtive look over his shoulder to Flynn's cell.

In response, she saluted. Suppressing a rueful smile, Ranzel followed his one-time master up the stairs.

Trapped in a cell, Flynn smiled. She saw the change in Ranzel. Zelroth wasn't his master anymore. Ranzel no longer needed one. He wasn't a *young one,* he wasn't an apprentice, he wasn't a pawn. He was a man. A mage in his own right. And

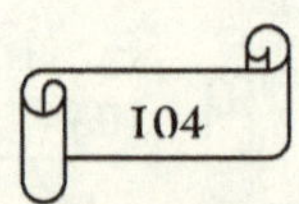

he was about to start acting like one because he'd picked a side in this magical war.

Flynn knew he would be there, fighting at her side. Now, to fully understand what they were fighting against.

# Chapter Eleven

IN THE DAYS THAT FOLLOWED, Ranzel surreptitiously gathered more information from Zelroth. At least he *tried* to. But the mage wouldn't tell him much more, and Ranzel gained a newfound sympathy for Flynn's reconnaissance efforts.

Ranzel had wanted to hear Zelroth's side of the story. To understand his master's reasoning and plans, but Zelroth was dismissive. The arrogant master could see no reason for Ranzel to have knowledge or opinions when all Zelroth needed was his apprentice's loyalty and power. Instead of looking for explanations, Ranzel began to look at actions—and Zelroth's actions were questionable at

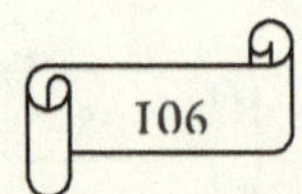

best. Locking a soldier in the tower? Denying her food? Manipulating Ranzel? Lying to him about the 'negotiations'?

A lifetime of questionable actions told Ranzel all he needed to know: Zelroth was wrong, and he needed to make it right.

For the first time, Ranzel used his magic as he wished and created a means to free Flynn. Once she was gone, he would face Zelroth. But first, he wanted her out of the cage and off the isle. Despite the food and water Ranzel snuck in, Flynn was weakening. Not in spirit, the soldier would never weaken in spirit. But physically she was suffering, and Ranzel couldn't stand it.

For her part, Flynn wasn't enjoying captivity. However, she *did* enjoy needling her captor. Zelroth had caged her in his workspace, so she figured it was her right to disrupt it.

"You know, Athaleen actually likes magic users," she said one day, her voice pitched to a loud, annoying volume. "I suppose they probably don't like *you*, not after what you did to their princes, but, generally speaking, they like magic users."

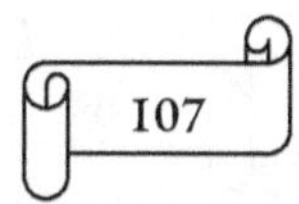

"But they do not revere," the mage responded, surprising Flynn.

Until now, he had easily and religiously ignored her every comment. She'd given him a history of Athaleen, explained to him the detailed anatomy of a water bat, told him her views on the existence of merpeople, and detailed what made a bow truly great. She'd even taunted him with the fact that he'd been beaten by two women and voiced her opinions on women's superiority as fighters.

Yet, Zelroth never engaged.

Still, Princess Flynn spoke on.

She rather liked her own company. Over time, she had come to suspect Zelroth took potions to drown her out. It seemed Zelroth had a potion for everything.

In one of her silent moments, Flynn had watched him cataloging his potions, reciting the names aloud.

"Bone healing. Check. Skin healing. Check. Ward Creator. Check. Insect Repellent. Check. Royalty repellent. Double check."

The list had gone on and on. Flynn commented on the vast assortment, but the mage hadn't replied. But

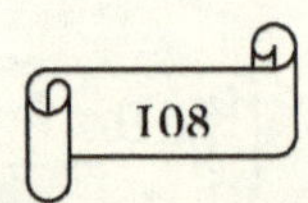

that was yesterday, and today he was speaking. He was *engaging*.

Not about to pass up the chance to chat, Flynn replied, "Why should *you* be revered? Shouldn't reverence be earned?"

"And is that what your precious royalty does?" he asked, refusing to turn her direction, leaving her to communicate with his back. "Earn your loyalty?"

"Actually, yes," Flynn said, recalling the times her father had proven himself as an amazing king, balancing family demands and kingdom needs.

"You are a foolish, foolish one, little soldier." Zelroth strode to his desk, his robes billowing behind him. Looking at a letter he had just penned, he said, "I believe I have finally found a use for you. But because you are loyal, I assume you will need convincing." That being said, the mage perused his potions as Flynn looked on with undisguised interest.

With a triumphant grunt, the mage snatched up a revolting greenish colored potion, mixed one drop of it into a small vial filled with water, moved to her cell, and splashed the potion on Flynn's leg.

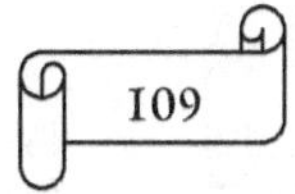

The pain and shock were instant. It was the stinging prick of a thousand bees and the throbbing pressure of a dozen strikes. Unprepared for the attack, Flynn couldn't help herself and screamed in pain. She grabbed at her leg. Tears streamed down her face. She gasped, trying to breathe through the agony.

All the while, Zelroth stood over her cage, his beady eyes protruding in glee as he watched her suffer.

The moment the pain receded, he pulled a vial from a pouch and poured it down the edge of her cage. The metal parted, and she was free. However, the mage threw another potion at the injured soldier. This one made Flynn groggy. Her movements slowed, and her body became very weak. So weak that the mage was able to pull her from the cell and set her at the desk without a struggle—Flynn's only struggle was keeping herself upright.

Zelroth's putrid breath poured over her as he forced a quill into her hand, saying, "Draw me the footprint of your palace, list the rotation of the guards, and tell me where the secret entrance is."

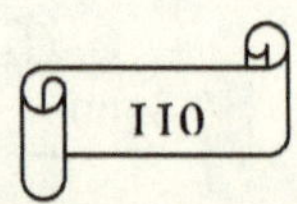

"I thought you had a traitor already in place," Flynn forced the words past her fumbling lips.

"I don't have time to wait for his correspondence. The winds are changing. Now tell me," Zelroth said, shaking her like a rag.

"Never," Flynn said. She wanted the word to come out strong, a resounding, fiery shout. Instead, she garbled it, the effects of the potions making her mouth soft. She may have even drooled.

Master Zelroth didn't retaliate. He only leaned closer, his yellow teeth flashing as he snarled, "One drop. I only used one drop."

Then, Zelroth threw her back in the cage, pushed the bars closed, and poured a potion over them to seal her in. Moving to the desk, he mixed another dropper of the vial potion and set it on the table. Ensuring she could see the concoction, he moved to the door. "I'm going to give you one hour to reconsider," he said.

Then he left.

The effects of the second potion faded away as Flynn lay in despair. How would she cope? She was about to give in to the tears gathering in her eyes

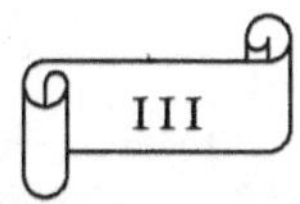

when Ranzel snuck into the room. He rushed to her side.

"I heard you," he said, his voice a pained echo of her despair. Reaching his hand through the bars, he laid it on her head. "Where do I need to heal you?" he asked.

"Nowhere. The pain disappeared. It's gone," she said, embarrassed. She hopped to her feet and spun around to show she was fine.

"You will be gone, too," he said. He pulled a potion from his pocket and opened her cell using the same method as Zelroth. "You have to leave. Run," he demanded, pushing her toward the hidden door.

"What? I can't leave. I'm sure with all his potions, he'll find me on the isle. And what will he do to you when he finds out you helped me?" The arguments spilt from Flynn's lips. "And you—"

"He won't find out, Flynn." Ranzel grinned recklessly. "Because I'm going to *become* you."

"No," Flynn said, and this time the word came out as strong and forceful as she wished.

"It's the perfect plan, Flynn," Ranzel said, and reached for her hand. She pulled it from his reach.

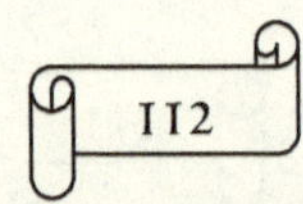

"You will run," he continued, "I will pretend to be you *and* be me. We're never in the same place at the same time. Zelroth will never know. You'll hide out on the isle, wait until your people come. The winds are changing. They should be here any day. Then you leave. Once you're gone, I'll stop pretending to be you. Zelroth will know you've escaped, but it will be too late. You'll be safe. There's only one problem..."

"That you're crazy!? That you'll be tortured? That you're talking so much and it's very, very out of character. So out of character it's scaring me!" Flynn hissed at him, pulling the door shut on her cell and shutting Ranzel outside.

He gently pried the door open, dragging her a few inches across the floor as she tried to hold it closed. His voice strained with the effort of their tug-of-war, he said, "Talking is necessary, not a problem. The *problem* is the tether."

"What?" Flynn snapped. Her surprise gave Ranzel the upper hand. He grabbed her arm and yanked her out of the cell, pulling her to him. "Do you trust me enough to wear this tether?" He held up a simple

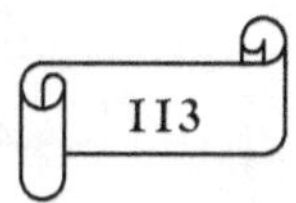

bracelet made of leather. A tiny pendant was secured inside it.

Flynn looked from Ranzel to the tether, then back again.

"Please, Flynn," Ranzel said, realizing with his inexperience at rambling, he hadn't yet explained this part. "This tether allows me to sense your proximity to me, that's all. If you wear it, I'll know when you're gone. I'll know when the charade is up."

"But…the torture," she argued, refusing to accept this plan.

"I won't be tortured," he reasoned. "I can just give him false information."

"I wouldn't give in that easily," she said in a low tone.

Silence fell as Ranzel accepted the truth. To play a convincing Flynn, he would have to endure the horrible potion. "What's a little torture, when you're a talented physical mage?" he said. "I'll hurt and I'll heal. And you'll be safe."

"Why are you doing this?" Flynn said, hoping that if she stalled long enough, Ranzel would be forced to

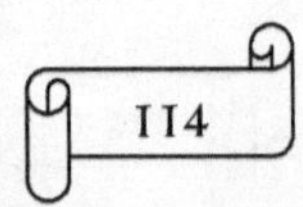

give up this crazy idea, or she could change his mind, or…

"I'm doing this because someone has to warn Athaleen. And that someone has to be you." He paced away from her and back. Shaking his head, he stepped into her personal space, placed his hands gently on her shoulders, and said, "No, that's not true. You'll do this for Athaleen. I'll do this for you."

"Ran—"

Ranzel interrupted her protest with a soft kiss to her forehead. Easing away, he smiled into her wide, shocked eyes. "Please, Flynn. I'm asking you. Please, for me. I can't stand to see you hurt. I—"

"No," she said, even more force behind the word than the last time. "You will wait to finish that sentence. We'll have this conversation when we're not in a dingy cell, and I'm not smelling like a carcass." She snatched the bracelet from his hand and stared at it, holding the pendant to the light. "You made this before he threatened me," she realized.

"I've been planning for this, Flynn. It isn't a thrown-together act of desperation. This can work. This *will* work. Please trust that this is the best

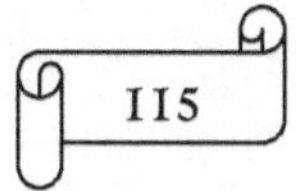

option. Please trust me," he said, pleading, practically begging.

Flynn broke. "I will," she said, shoving the bracelet over her hand. "And I'm happy to wear your tether, to keep a connection with you. Be well," she whispered before giving Ranzel one last fierce hug and a resounding kiss on the cheek.

Unwilling to let him see her cry, Flynn turned away as he locked himself in the cell and she escaped the tower.

# Chapter Twelve

FLYNN RAN THROUGH THE TREES, swinging wildly at the branches barring her path. Her movements were erratic. She weaved through the forest, stumbling as if the potion was still affecting her coordination. It wasn't. Her poor coordination was a mark of her indecision.

After days of captivity and inactivity, Flynn needed to move. But she wasn't convinced she was moving in the right direction.

The further she got from Ranzel, the more chaotic her churning steps became. Narrowly missing a tree, she bumped into another. Off balance, she fell to her knees. Frantically, she regained her feet and ran on as

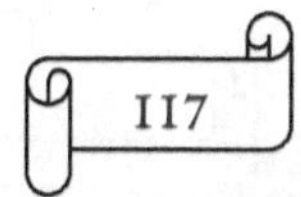

if being chased by a monster. But the only monster nipping at her heels was her guilt. She had left Ranzel with a madman.

She had left.

The cliff stopped her, forced her to face her choice. Her hands on her knees, she stood gasping, staring out over the sea. There was no sail in sight, no salvation there to be found, no army coming to attack, no leader coming to tell her what to do.

Every choice felt wrong. Putting one mage's life before her entire kingdom? Treacherous. Leaving her family in danger? Unthinkable. Abandoning Ranzel? A betrayal.

Flynn dropped to her knees, heedless of the cold earth. What should she do? What *could* she do? She was a lone soldier, a foolish adventurer, a hidden princess.

The consequences of her actions were paralyzing. Gasping for breath, she cried to the Maker. *Why?* She repeated the question over and over, leaning back on her heels to raise her face to heaven. As she did, air filled her hungry lungs, satisfying her body's needs. The pain in her chest eased, her thoughts settled.

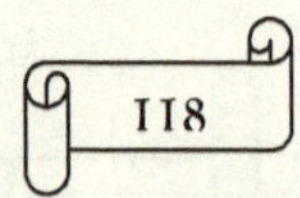

She had stumbled onto a horrible threat to her kingdom. She had learned so much about magic. About herself. She'd found the mage who'd cursed her brothers, Zelroth. She'd found Ranzel.

Ranzel. The best consequence of all.

With a shock of clarity, Flynn saw the Maker's interventions. He'd brought her here. Her. Flynn. And he trusted her to make the right choice, to follow the truth He put in her heart. She wasn't a lone soldier; she was a well-trained fighter. She wasn't a foolish adventurer; she was a determined explorer. She wasn't a hidden royal; she was a bold princess. And princesses didn't run.

"Princesses don't run," she whispered as she recalled running through the palace, her mother's voice chiding her as she chased her siblings. She was Athaleen royalty. She had the strength of her kingdom, the power of her family's legacy behind her.

Leaning back, Flynn threw her arms wide and screamed, "PRINCESSES DON'T RUN!"

The wind snapped away her words, taking them out to sea.

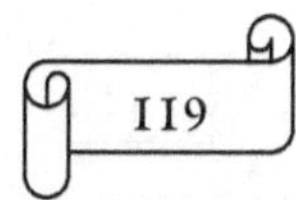

With a confident smile, Flynn rose, turned, and made her way back to the tower. Her steps were sure, her path straight.

Because princesses didn't run.

RANZEL HAD BEEN OVERLY CONFIDENT. Holding the appearance of another was easy under regular circumstances. Under pressure, it was harder, but while being tortured, it was almost impossible.

He pinched his lips together, holding back a scream.

Zelroth stood over him, looking almost bored with the proceedings. Of course, he didn't realize he was hurting his pet mage, but even so, he thought he was torturing a young girl! Zelroth was evil, disturbed. Wrong. How had Ranzel ever thought he was right? As the pain receded, Zelroth pulled another potion from his pocket and tossed it at Ranzel.

And that's when everything went wrong.

The potion was the same as the one Zelroth had used to weaken Flynn. But it did more than debilitate. It lessened a person's ability to control

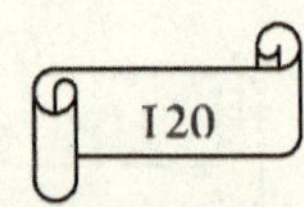

their physical body—or to maintain the form of someone else's.

"Ranzel!?" Zelroth said in utter disbelief as his prisoner morphed before his eyes. Zelroth may have been evil, but he wasn't stupid. Instantly, he realized what had happened. Grabbing Ranzel by the front of his tunic, he hauled him to his feet. "What have you done, boy!?"

"Stopped you," Ranzel said in a weak voice, but he allowed for his disdain of the master to show in his eyes.

"You'll never stop me," Zelroth hissed, not realizing how foolish it was to lay out such a challenge—especially when a certain princess listened at the door.

In a raging fit, Zelroth threw his impaired apprentice to the floor. "Betray me! After all I have done for you. Snatching you from the gutter. I should have known better, left you to die where you belong! But now you will pay!" He rushed to the work table, grabbing the deadly vial.

"No!" Ranzel said, scrambling clumsily away from the livid mage. He knew the power of that potion.

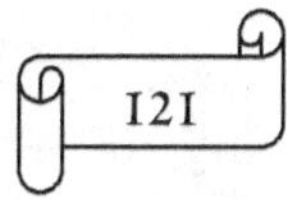

Knew the intent was to kill him in the most horrible way possible.

In his panic, Ranzel called to a Maker, he'd never reached for before. He closed his eyes, praying his death would be quick, praying Flynn would escape.

Vial in hand, Zelroth stalked toward the cage.

"Stop!" Flynn screamed, stepping through the wooden door. Zelroth froze. Not because of Flynn's windswept, breathless appearance, or even her shouted demand. The master froze because the stored vials were…glowing.

The vials of power Zelroth had stolen by syphoning power from the royals were reacting to Flynn's return. Those potions packed with the power of royalty—a power activated by a royal's protective instincts and their willing sacrifice—were vibrantly shining, row upon row lit as if it were a flame.

Zelroth stepped away from Ranzel, moving toward Flynn with a gleeful stride. "You're a princess."

Flynn stared at the bottles, realizing her instinct to protect Ranzel had given her away. Straightening her shoulders, she said, "I am."

"Perfect," Zelroth said before lunging.

Flynn dodged through the door, slamming it on the mage's hand. He howled in pain, flinging the door open in rage.

Flynn was already up the stairs, her mind flipping through methods of escape. The window? No, it was too far down. She'd have to find a way around Zelroth, grab Ranzel, and run for it out the hidden door.

Sprinting through the main tower room—her and Ranzel's makeshift sparring ground—she saw it; her bow. Zelroth had stripped her of it on her initial capture, but Ranzel had returned it to her usual storage space. Dashing past, she snatched up the bow and nearby quiver.

In the glass garden, she scrambled up a tree, perched, and waited. When Zelroth cleared the last stair, she was ready. Her shot landed perfectly, the arrow striking Zelroth's shoulder. Flynn didn't want to kill the mage, not when there were still so many secrets. Not when they still knew so little about The Sentinels. But she, most certainly, wanted to wound him.

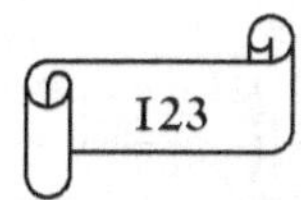

He cried out in pain and dropped to a knee. With one hand splayed painfully on the ground and the other clutching the arrow, he glared at the princess.

"Move to the center of the room and put your hands over your head," Flynn demanded. "Or this next arrow will go through your heart."

"What a nasty, little princess you are," Zelroth said, pulling a shaking leg under him to stand. "You seem to think you have the upper hand here."

"As does the arrow sticking out of your arm," Flynn said with a brittle smile.

Zelroth reached up, grabbed the arrow, and pulled it free. Blood spread from the wound to his robe, but he ignored it, saying, "Better?"

"I thought it suited you," Flynn said with a sly smirk. She motioned with her drawn bow. "Now, move to the center of the room."

"I have a better idea," the master said, and with surprising quickness, darted for the stairs.

Flynn's arrow bounced off the wall above his head as he sprinted away. She launched herself from the tree and raced after him. A sickening premonition of Zelroth's plan rushed her feet down the curving

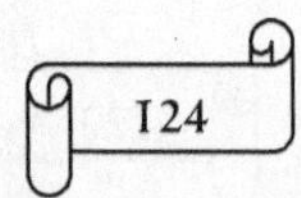

stairs of the tower. As she reached the top of the last set of stairs, the scene before her stopped her in her tracks.

She had been right. Zelroth was once again using his apprentice to get what he wanted. Flynn had always enjoyed being right, but this time, she greatly disliked it…and she disliked Zelroth even more.

In one hand, the evil mage clutched the back of Ranzel's shirt. In the other, he held the torturing potion above Ranzel's head. "Now, dear princess," he said, his words tight with packed sarcasm, "now, you see, I have always had the upper hand."

# Chapter Thirteen

DARKNESS FILLED THE ROOM, but it was unspoken words that filled the cage.

Ranzel huddled in one corner, staring listlessly into the void. The metal bars and tower walls surrounded him, locking him in, but Ranzel was used to being hidden away. He'd lived most of his life locked away, hidden from the world. But he wasn't a fool.

He knew the precariousness of this situation, knew his faults and sins, and he now knew Flynn—a princess!—would never stay by his side. She deserved better. Whether princess or soldier, she always had.

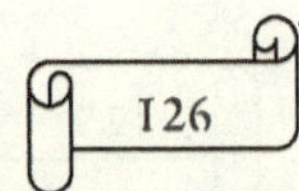

Flynn sat cross-legged in their cage, her own racing thoughts plaguing her peace. She was planted in the middle of the cell facing Ranzel, but unable to see his face. Unable to read his expression, all she could read was the silence.

It didn't give her much hope.

"Ranzel," she began, her voice tentative. "I'm sorry. I wish I could have told you. I wish I would have. You deserved to know."

"I deserve very little," Ranzel mumbled.

"What? What do you mean?" Flynn said, shifting a tiny bit closer to him in the dark. She'd expected anger. *She* would've been angry. But that was the best thing about Ranzel, he wasn't like her. He wasn't like anyone. He was courage and safety and acceptance all blended together.

"I'm a street urchin, Flynn," he grumbled. His voice was muted, lacking hope. "Unwanted by my kingdom," he sighed, "and you're a princess. Honored by your kingdom. We are not the same." He turned his head, his words directed away from her. "We will never be the same. We will never belong together, much less in the same place."

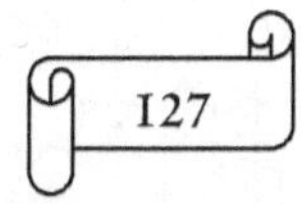

"Ranzel, I am a princess who was at home in your tower. Who is at home in her fancy suite at the palace. Who is at home here in this cell. I belong where I decide I belong." Flynn filled her proclamation with power. Leaning forward onto her knees, she continued, "And you do too. You can belong in Athaleen. With me…If you want it."

"Your brothers…your parents." Ranzel shuddered, his mind conjuring up a room full of angry royals. "A king," he whispered in a voice full of fear and disbelief. He couldn't face her family, couldn't face a *king*.

Flynn purposely ignored his awe of her royal family and focused on the details, saying, "My brothers will forgive any involvement you had in creating the tethers. You. Didn't. Know. My parents, the king…well, they just want me to be fulfilled. To find my purpose in life."

"It can't be me, Flynn." Ranzel's fingers grazed hers in the darkness. She turned her fingers, hoping he was reaching to clasp her hand.

But he wasn't. He was searching for the tether on her wrist. The last thing that bound her to him. When

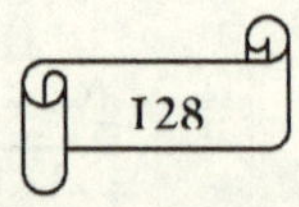

he found it, he pulled, trying to free it from her wrist. Flynn clapped her hand over it.

"No, Ranzel."

"Give me the tether, Flynn."

"No."

A struggle ensued, and somehow, at the end of it, Flynn had pinned Ranzel to the dingy cell floor.

With her knees to one side of him, she loomed over his chest, her arms forcing his into the packed earthen floor. She leaned closer to him, close enough he could see the flash of her beautiful eyes in the meager light. Her jaw was firm, her gaze intense. "I'm no longer making choices to please other people, Ranzel. So, I don't really care what they think. I know I'm in the right. Saving you was *my* choice. *You* are my choice," she said, her tone threatening in an affectionate way. "I know you. I accept *all* of you. Good and bad. We are in this together, and there's no one. *No one,* I'd rather fight with."

"How can we ever belong together, a princess and rogue mage?" Ranzel whispered, his voice quiet with despair.

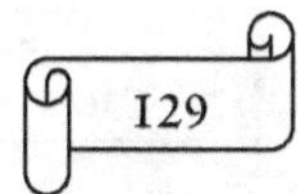

"We're already tethered, my dear mage." Flynn inched close enough to whisper in Ranzel's ear. "And you care for me. You've sacrificed for me. And I trust you." It seemed simple enough to Flynn. Choose to fight together now, embrace the affection growing between them, escape the isle, and create a true love.

Ranzel continued to argue, saying, "I just don't—"

She threw herself back, holding him at arm's length. "You don't care for me? Don't find me attractive covered in my prison stench?"

"Of course, I do," Ranzel impulsively answered. He couldn't be anything but honest with Flynn. He never wanted to lie again, especially to her.

Flynn grinned, and her smile was so wide, Ranzel could feel its impact. Her joy hurt. He might be the cause of it now, in this horrible cell, but he couldn't give her that joy forever. He had nothing but regret to give.

"Flynn," he pleaded, "You deserve more. I have nothing—"

"You are everything."

"You'll be—"

"Happy."

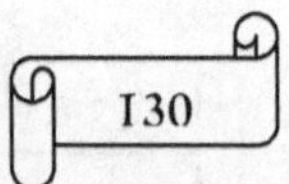

"Not in the future. Then you'll be sad. And poor and—"

Seeing her words were no longer convincing, Flynn decided on a different way of convincing Ranzel. She was less sure of this method, considering she had massive amounts of practice speaking but much, much less practice kissing.

Still, as she pressed her lips to Ranzel's, she felt a conviction that struck her to her core. Ranzel belonged with her, and she belonged with him.

Ranzel reacted quickly, kissing Flynn back. Initially, he planned a quick kiss, one to remember their connection by, but—like every moment since she had stumbled through the window of his tower—Flynn's presence drew him in. He couldn't set her aside. He couldn't deny he was better at her side. He didn't deserve her, but he'd protect her till the day he died. He would *love* her until he died—which would probably be far too soon.

With that depressing realization, Ranzel pulled Flynn closer, but softened his kiss. When he pulled away, Flynn peppered Ranzel's face with kisses as he laughed reluctantly. When Flynn eased away, Ranzel

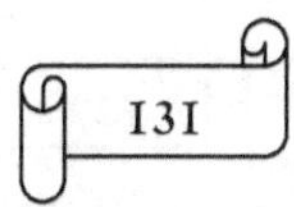

kept one hand buried in her hair and the other splayed across her back. "I thought there was to be no talk of love while prisoners," he said, giving in to a smirk.

"Desperate times," she said, smiling down on him.

He returned her smile, but then his slowly faded, and he said, "These *are* desperate times. Zelroth will use us. He'll use us indefinitely." Ranzel's hands tightened their hold, pulling Flynn closer to him as if he could protect her with his will alone. He continued, "All he has to do is threaten me with some wild animal, engage your protective instincts to fight, have you kill the creature, and release your royal magic. Then he can make more and more of his precious potion."

Flynn slowly moved away from Ranzel and sat, sliding to her back to the wall of the cell. "I have a plan," she said, "but you'll need to learn a new trick, my magician."

"I'm a mage, not a magician," Ranzel said grumpily, as he moved to sit beside his princess.

"Sure you are," she said, waving his offense away. If she could joke about the quirks of royalty, he could

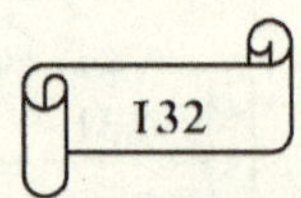

learn to be teased about the quirks of being a magic user.

Flynn placed her hand in Ranzel's and shifted until it was nestled comfortably before continuing. "Now, you say you heal by pushing the pain and injury from your body. Do you think you could activate that magic before the injury, creating a kind of barrier?"

"I don't know," Razel mused. It sounded feasible. It *should* work. It needed to work.

ZELROTH RUBBED HIS HANDS TOGETHER in anticipatory glee. What a gift his deceiving young apprentice had given him. A princess. An endless fountain of power, and a way to get her to use it. It was perfect. It was—

Loud.

Opening the door to his potion room, he heard the princess wailing in the corner. "Please, please," she blubbered. "Something is wrong with Ranzel." She hiccupped, crying sloppy tears—the weak royalty in her veins on display.

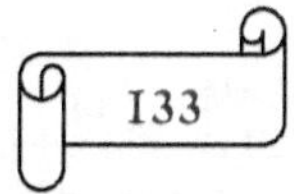

"Hurry, he isn't moving, and he won't wake up!" She whined some more.

Zelroth knew a trick when he saw one. These two idiots were no match for his superior…well, superior everything.

Rifling through his potions, he found the dancing one. It had been a discarded idea. An idea to force princesses to dance endlessly. It would have been amusing, but unhelpful to his cause. Tapping a drop into a stopper, he mixed in some water. The last thing he needed was a forever dancing mage.

This mixture ought to give him a few minutes, enough time to prove Ranzel was actually well and Zelroth wasn't an idiot.

All the while, the princess cried in the corner like a mourner at a funeral. Weeping and wailing, the tears of a lesser, weak human.

Without ceremony, Zelroth strode to the cage and dumped the potion on Ranzel.

Nothing happened. Not a twitch of a dancing leg or jig of an arm.

Zelroth rushed to open the metal door, pouring the dissolving potion down the bar. He tossed a

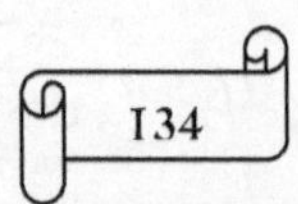

disabling potion at the sobbing princess—who was collapsed at the gate of the door—and pushed her hastily out of the way. Dropping to his knees before his apprentice, he felt for a pulse.

A hand shot out, grabbing his wrist. Zelroth reached his free hand toward the potion at his belt, but that movement was stopped by a strong grip.

"You've always underestimated me, Zelroth," Ranzel said, standing and pinning the mage's hands together.

"And you've always underestimated me!" With that, Zelroth kicked out, catching the disabled princess in the stomach.

Flynn groaned in pain, and Ranzel's hold momentarily loosened. The master's next kick sent Ranzel sprawling against the bars, but he recovered fast enough to stop the mage from accessing a potion.

With a quick motion, Ranzel yanked at the belt at his master's waist, sending his array of potions to the ground. The hours of training with Flynn paid off as the princess lay incapacitated, and he faced his master. With another blistering movement, he punched Zelroth.

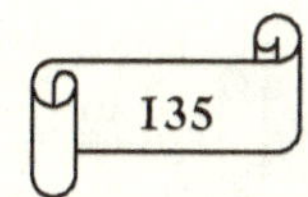

The impact sent Zelroth tripping over Flynn and out of the cage. The soldier-princess curled more tightly into a ball, attempting to avoid further injury as she fought the effects of the potion.

"Flynn?" Ranzel asked as stepped past her and out of the cage. He refused to take his eyes off Zelroth or stop in his pursuit of the mage, but needed to know his princess's injuries weren't extreme.

"Get…him," Flynn sputtered, and Ranzel continued his advance on Zelroth.

With a crazed energy, the master attacked. With deliberate control, the apprentice counterattacked. Around the potion room, their battle traveled. Potions littered the floor as they were knocked from shelves, but landing in the soft dirt, none shattered.

Until Ranzel stepped on one.

At the crack of the glass, a flaming orange mist rose and hovered around Ranzel for an instant before absorbing into him.

With a surge of power, Ranzel shot forward, landing a hard blow on his master. Zelroth fell, his arms flying high in the air as he arched to the ground.

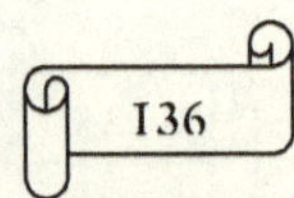

The master landed in a crumpled heap, dirt puffing around him as his head lolled to the side.

The instant Ranzel registered his opponent's unconscious state, he rushed to Flynn.

The princess had dragged her uncooperative body to the table and was searching through Zelroth's potions. "I know it was here. Bright, bright red. Where is it?" Her hands fumbled.

"Here!" Ranzel said, finding it instantly and holding it up in victory.

Flynn met his eyes and froze. "What happened to you?" she whisper-hissed. "You look so…"

"Powerful," Ranzel said, "it was a potion, I feel…odd. Absolute clarity. Total strength. Everything is amplified."

"Well, you look scary," Flynn said. Seeing Ranzel's face fall, she amended her statement. "Scary, but handsome. Very handsome." She made a very awkward move toward the hidden door—leaning heavily on the table—and said, "Let's get out of here."

"You're sure this is it?" Ranzel asked, eying the potion.

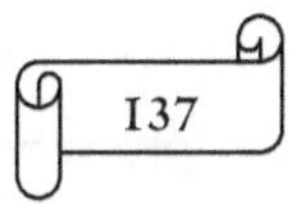

Flynn paused her pathetic movements and studied Ranzel's expression. "Yes," she said. Ranzel had seemed okay with this part of her plan at first, but it was...extreme. "Yes," she repeated, "that's the explosive one. It will probably start a chain reaction and destroy everything. Are you sure this is what you want? I know, the tower, it—"

"No, it needs to happen." With determination and a sharp, angry move, Ranzel lifted his arm to pull the stopper from the potion. Physically and mentally prepared, he instructed Flynn to get the hidden door open, saying, "Hold it for me, and be ready to run."

Adrenaline seemed to clear the remainder of the potion from Flynn's veins, and she rushed to access the door with controlled movements. "Now, Ranzel!" she yelled as the door creaked open, sunlight flooding into the tower basement.

"NO!" Zelroth screamed.

The master was on his feet, his pouch of potions in hand. "They will never accept you, Ranzel! Never!" He leaned precariously to one side, but continued his advance upon his apprentice. "We have worked too hard. Been set aside too long. They will hate you, but

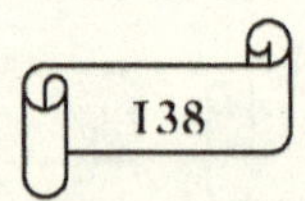

I never will. We will put this behind us." He lurched to a stop, holding an entreating hand out to Ranzel. "I will accept you. I will accept your magic."

Flynn watched the scene, feeling uncharacteristically passive. She trusted Ranzel. Trusted in his belief in her and their future.

"That's the only part of me you love," Ranzel said, voice heavy with emotion. He stared at his master's outstretched hand and remembered the boy who'd clung to the master like a lifeline. The boy who had trusted the wrong mage, but was now a wiser man. Clutching the explosive potion in a sweaty palm, Ranzel continued, "You've only ever wanted my magic. You don't want me to think, but to just provide a power that you can direct and shape as you please. Well, I deserve to be more than my magic. I—"

Zelroth's other hand twitched, throwing a disabling potion at Ranzel.

Ranzel remained unmoving. But he wasn't in shock. He had protected himself. Having finally accepted just how evil his master was, he was prepared for this attack.

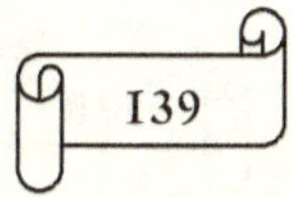

As the potion splashed against his magical shield, Ranzel just raised a disapproving eyebrow at the mage. Then, without a word, he flung the potion past Zelroth's dirty, grasping fingers to the far side of the room, sprinted to a wildly gesturing Flynn, and left his past behind.

# Chapter Fourteen

HAND IN HAND, Ranzel and Flynn ran from the tower. At least they did until Flynn realized holding hands greatly hampered a person's ability *to* run. With Ranzel keeping pace, Flynn dropped his hand and raced forward. Arms pumping freely, they sped effectively away from the tower and into the nearby forest.

Anxiety pushed the pair's pace. Catastrophe seemed close, the explosion of potions imminent.

The mage and the princess sprinted on, making it some distance into the trees before stopping. Their lungs burned, and their legs moved restlessly as they cowered in the cover of the forest. Backs scraping

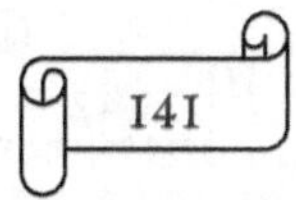

against a large oak, they waited for the earth-shattering explosion.

It didn't come.

Fear did. Fear came in the silence of the unknown. Flynn's eyes grew bright with dreadful anticipation while Ranzel's darkened with grim determination.

Without a word, they both rose and peered cautiously around the tree. They inched forward, craning their necks for a view of the tower through the forest. With their gasping breaths the only sound on the isle, they strained to see, to hear, to discover the fate of the master, Zelroth.

Then, they saw him racing from the tower.

Had Zelroth found a way to stop the explosion? Could he possibly have a potion for even that? Flynn felt an unfamiliar feeling creep up on her: despair. For a moment, tears pricked at her eyes, and her lungs seized. But then she noted the frenzy of Zelroth's movements, the panic.

His arms were loaded with potions. He wasn't rushing to attack. He wasn't fleeing from the imminent destruction. He dropped an armful of vials on the grass and rushed back to the tower.

Disregarding the danger, Zelroth was foolishly trying to save the royal potions.

Ranzel made a move to follow Zelroth, but stopped himself with a sorrowful shake of his head. Flynn clutched his arm, seconds from restraining him. If Ranzel had attempted to endanger his life for his master, she would have tackled him without hesitation, but she was grateful to see that he finally, finally valued his life over Zelroth's.

Still, Flynn clung to Ranzel, afraid he would change his mind. Afraid his goodness wouldn't allow him to stand by and let Zelroth choose his fate. Afraid of his heroics.

In turn, Ranzel clung to a tree, the bark digging into his powerful hands. He was afraid, too. Afraid the potions wouldn't explode, and afraid that they would.

Then, suddenly—but also finally—came the first explosion. It was small, a rumble and a burst of color from the tower windows. A pause followed, but no master appeared.

Zelroth didn't heed the tower's warning.

The second and final explosion was massive.

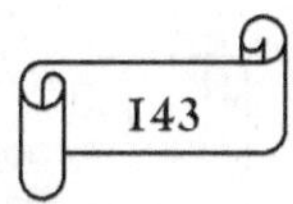

The destruction multiplied, turning into a rainbow of colorful smoke and a pounding, shaking vibration.

Ranzel and Flynn fell to the damp, quaking earth. Hands over their ears, they watched the tower quake and falter under the magical attack. It gave way suddenly, like water crashing through a dam. Toppling over, the stone crashed to the ground, a pile of rubble.

The mage and princess remained unmoving as the dust settled and the isle quieted.

They remained unmoving as Ranzel processed the loss. The loss of his home. The loss of his master. The loss of his innocence as he accepted that his master had never loved him. His master had only loved Ranzel's power, and he had only wanted more and more power. More magic. So much that he died for it.

Flynn pinched her lips closed and stayed still, one hand on Ranzel's shoulder. She had so much to say, even more than she usually did, but now wasn't the time.

There would be time later to tell Ranzel he was brave. He was impressive. He was more than his

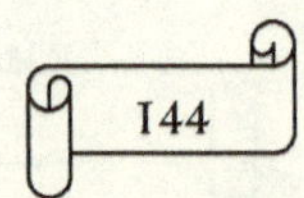

magic. He was who she wanted on every one of her adventures, every time.

Silently, they dug through the rubble. Quietly, they buried Zelroth. Without words, they gathered their few surviving things and set up a camp. It wasn't until dusk had fallen and a fire was burning that Ranzel spoke.

"I'm glad," he said, tossing tiny bits of a twig into the flame.

Flynn stopped fiddling with her hair and joined him, sitting on the grass. She leaned her head on his shoulder, knowing he was ready for connection. "What makes you glad?" she asked, her voice drifting over the flames, filling the void of a quiet finally broken.

"You," Ranzel answered without hesitation, "and how it all ended. I'm glad that part of my life is over. Glad that Zelroth chose his own fate. Glad that you're safe."

Flynn beamed and snuggled in closer to him, linking her arms around his. "I'm glad I'm safe, too," she said. Ranzel laughed softly, and Flynn sighed in quiet pleasure.

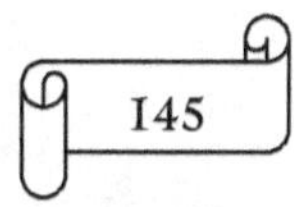

He was happy. She had been worried he would be sad, broken. But he wasn't. He was glad and—

"I'm scared," he admitted.

Flynn jerked away from him. "Scared?! Of what?" Flynn was rarely scared. She didn't have much time for fear, but here on the isle she had felt it. She had felt it when she was injured, had felt it when Ranzel was discovered helping her, had felt it almost take her to her knees when she thought her plan would fail.

Yes, here she had learned fear. Learned to fear in all new, terrible ways. But right now, she was anything but afraid.

"As royalty—"

"That horrible royalty," Flynn interrupted with a teasing smile.

"The best royal I know," Ranzel said and kissed her forehead. Flynn was too busy melting to point out that he knew no other royals.

"As a princess, a soldier, a valued citizen of Athaleen," Ranzel continued, "I know you're not scared of it, but I am. I'm scared of the future. Where do I belong?"

Flynn moved to her knees in front of him and framed his hands in her face. "Ranzel, the future is the best part," she said, her eyes glowing with bright anticipation. "Because it *is* unknown. Because it *is* exciting. Because I love you!"

She pinched her lips together, shocked at her own admission. Of course, she felt it, but saying it made it real. Looking at Ranzel's bright eyes, she felt no regret. She had found what Tesha and Humphrey had—a relationship with amazing fulfillment. She laughed aloud and said, "Yes! Because I love you. Because of everything we'll get to discover. Because we'll discover it together. Because of you!"

By the time she was finished, Ranzel was laughing too because Flynn punctuated each sentence with a small, forceful kiss to his cheeks. "So," she said, trying not to smile, "it will be great, because I will not stand for it to be anything but!" This sentence, she punctuated with a long, meaningful kiss.

Such a meaningful kiss, that Ranzel and Flynn quit talking again for quite some time. It was amazing, actually, that after Zelroth's betrayal, Ranzel trusted in the princess's assurances so completely, but he

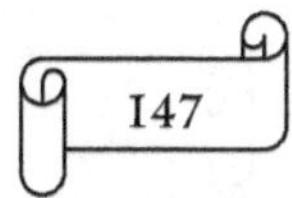

did. Flynn had guaranteed his future would be positive, exciting.

And Ranzel trusted Flynn. So much so that he made a new vow. A better vow. One more heartfelt than any he had ever given his master.

"Princess Flynn," he said, "to you my magic, and my love, is freely given."

RANZEL WAS WISE TO TRUST FLYNN. And he became even wiser as he began to trust himself. She brought him confidence, and he gave her peace. In that confidence and peace, they found faith and happiness. Yes, Flynn was right. The future *was* exciting.

On the most exciting, life-altering day of his life, Ranzel Nulla stood in the throne room of Athaleen next to his favorite princess-soldier as they listened to the king make a historic proclamation.

"The kingdom of Athaleen has long maintained a neutral stance regarding magic and magic usage. But as it often happens, when we seek neutrality and don't take a stance, the stance is assumed. And many

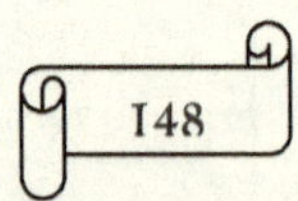

have wrongly assumed our stance on magic. With this proclamation, our stance will be made clear, and it is thus: all magic usage is allowed and even encouraged here on Athaleen. Like a weapon, magic can be used for good—to protect. Like a weapon, it can also be used for evil—to hurt. But the usage of it depends on the wielder. If magic is misused, there will be a punishment. But using it with training and respect for its dangers is welcome. If magic is found…"

Prince Humphrey, standing behind them, leaned forward, whispering to his sister, "Tesha wrote the greater portion of this." Anticipation lighting his countenance, the prince grinned across the throne room at his wife, Tesha, who stood at attention next to the other council members.

Tesha glared back at him, demanding good behavior with a look.

"It's brilliant," Flynn said. "Will she get credited for it?"

"She says it was created in council. And that what is discussed and agreed upon in council belongs to the kingdom," Humphrey said.

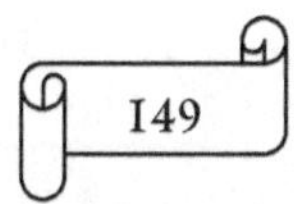

The prince looked particularly striking in a festive royal tunic. Anticipation lighting his countenance, he grinned at his wife, Tesha, who stood at attention across the throne room next to the other council members.

Tesha glared back at him, demanding good behavior with a look.

Flynn turned to Humphrey, feeling offended on Tesha's behalf. "I guess I will have to be sure she receives recognition for her brilliance."

"Why do you think I told you?" Humphrey winked at her smugly before snapping back to attention. Tesha returned her focus to the king, but Flynn noticed her stifle a smile.

Humphrey and Tesha had been amazingly supportive of Flynn upon her return to Athaleen with a mysterious mage. They'd praised her handling of an unconventional situation, her bravery in facing Zelroth, and her wisdom in building a relationship and understanding with Ranzel.

Their staunch faith in Flynn's judgment and choices had settled the king's reservations. Because of this, a closeness had built between the two

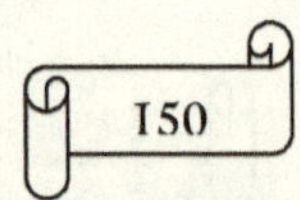

couples. A connection which greatly benefitted all involved.

Surrounded by so much love and support, Flynn beamed.

The king had moved on to making other, less brilliant announcements. Ranzel shifted nervously next to Flynn, and she squirmed in excitement, adjusting the skirt of her elegant, princess-like dress to lie just right.

Of course, Ranzel and Flynn were thrilled about the proclamation on magic, and any other day, it would have been the most anticipated announcement.

But not this day.

"As proof of our acceptance of magic and mages," the king said, and Flynn wriggled in place, smoothing her hair and swaying until Ranzel trapped her hand. Delighted, she linked her fingers with his.

King Maddox continued, "We have a very exciting announcement and an even more exciting event happening today." The king turned to smile upon Ranzel and Flynn. "My brave daughter Princess

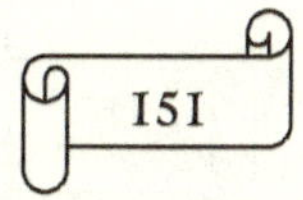

Flynn will be joining Mage Ranzel Nulla in matrimony this very day!"

Flynn jerked forward to join the king at the dais, practically dragging Ranzel behind. The mage followed in a daze. He still found it hard to believe the king and queen's support of their union. Remarkably, the royals had come to adore the quiet boy who not only made their daughter happy but made her better.

Determined to earn the trust of the kingdom as he had their princess, Ranzel quickened his steps until he was walking beside Flynn. She grinned up at him, so proud of her mage.

Yes, Flynn was right. The future was excitingly unexpected. Who knew what might happen, but he would be with Flynn. Always with Flynn. The mage and the princess-soldier.

# THE END

# Acknowledgments

I love the story of Rapunzel. A fairy tale with so much character growth that also showcases the strength to overcome—what's not too love? But I do have to admit, I had reservations about the writing of this story. Only two characters throughout the whole story? A lone tower? I wondered how I would make this story engaging and exciting. Luckily, these characters were so lovable. Their adventure built naturally. So, my first thanks goes to these great characters and the inspirational stories behind their tales.

Next, I need to thank my husband for giving me time and opportunity to create this book. You are amazing. Thanks for dreaming with me!

And thanks to my daughter who loved these characters first!

To Heather, who loved the characters enough to question them and make them better. I hope you like our more evolved Flynn! To Shalene and Wendy, who edited and ensured this story's heart shone through.

To all of my readers and author friends, thank you for the motivation to keep creating! May many great books be in your future!

And, of course, thanks to my Savior who gives me the inspiration and opportunity to tell uplifting stories that create and share light.

# About the Author

After living throughout the western U.S., Tenille now claims rural Northern Nevada as her home. If she's not reading or writing, she's enjoying a beautifully ordinary life with her amazing husband and four children. She loves the Lord and is grateful for the many opportunities she's discovered through serving Him. She strives to glorify Him by creating stories that entertain, uplift, and inspire.

Want to know more?
You can find her at www.tenilleberezay.com.

# Also by the Author

**The 12 Fighting Princes-Reversed Retellings Book 1**

Prince Humphrey enjoys fighting—fighting to outdo the soldiers in training, fighting to outsmart the king's strict rules, and fighting to outshine the first female captain of the guard. Humphrey enjoys it all, until...the curse. Being forced to fight is not particularly enjoyable, and being one of 12 princes forced to fight monster after monster, night after night, is absolutely terrible. Humphrey needs help—and surprisingly, it comes in the form of one determined captain.

**Dreamscape**

Nix is just a normal teenager, but her dreams are exceptional. Every night, she dreams of a fantasy world where she and her crew fight otherworldly monsters, confront mysterious threats, and face impossible quests. In the real world, Nix is caught up in things that seem simpler: forging her identity, building a romance, and maintaining old friendships. But as Nix's convictions are tested by an intense new relationship, the real world begins to feel more and more impossible. Desperate, Nix searches for direction, for confidence, for faith, for strength. And she finds it all in the most unlikely of places —her sleep.

**The Convergence-Converters Book 1**

Hiding unbelievable physical abilities, seventeen-year-old Desiree Morgan buries herself inside the realities of high school. But when Blake Thomas infiltrates her life, all of Desiree's secrets begin to unravel. With answers come more questions, and soon she is entangled in a world of secret societies, human experimentation, perilous power struggles, and ultimate sacrifice. To escape, Desiree can't be simply extraordinary...she must redefine the impossible.

**<u>The Keep</u>-Converters Book 2**

After a pardon from the convergence, Desiree returns to the protection of home. But safety is an illusion, and her family is shattered by the violent retribution of a desperate enemy. On the run again, Desiree struggles to keep those she loves from a host of gathering threats--debilitating doubts, manipulative converters, dark technology, and a murdering madman. To save them all, Desiree will need more than her ability to convert, she'll need to redefine her strength.

**<u>The Conclave</u>-Converters Book 3**

Having escaped the dangers of The Keep, Desiree is determined to free Blake. But when a government-enhanced converter goes rogue, the ensuing battle for power, control, and lives makes Blake's rescue a secondary mission. As Desiree struggles to overcome past demons and new, stifling expectations, she faces converters more powerful, dangerous, and desperate than ever. To protect those she loves, redeem the convergence, overtake The Keep, and honor her conclave, Desiree will have to redefine the future.

**The Café-Converters Book 0.5**

Living an absolutely ordinary life, Sarah works her way through college by earning money as a waitress at Café Columbia. When an unlikely connection is formed with one of her regulars, Sarah's life becomes anything but normal. As her new relationship develops, Sarah finds the strength to embrace an extraordinary life and, when tragedy strikes, to redefine her love.

www.ingramcontent.com/pod-product-compliance
Lightning Source LLC
LaVergne TN
LVHW090610110826
845146LV00001B/333

* 9 7 9 8 9 9 4 5 6 6 7 3 2 *